Books by PGM Simone

Yellow Cat

Children of the Crane

CHILDREN
of the
CRANE

by George Simone

iUniverse, Inc.
Bloomington

Children of the Crane

iUniverse books may be ordered through booksellers or by contacting:

iUniverse
1663 Liberty Drive
Bloomington, IN 47403
www.iuniverse.com
1-800-Authors (1-800-288-4677)

Because of the dynamic nature of the Internet, any web addresses or links contained in this book may have changed since publication and may no longer be valid.

ISBN: 978-1-4502-8873-6 (pbk)
ISBN: 978-1-4502-8874-3 (ebk)

Printed in the United States of America

iUniverse rev. date: 1/22/11

For Barbara

CONTENTS

1

Arrival

Porto dos Santos, São Paulo, Brasil

1908

A puff of smoke, a speck on the horizon, and a shout: "The *Kasato Maru* is here!"

The crowd surges forward, pushing a young man off the dock and into the water, where, against all odds, he lands unharmed among the spires of jagged rocks. Someone drops a rope, and a cluster of bystanders, glad for the diversion after a long wait, pulls the young man up.

His girlfriend kisses him and then, to the enthusiastic applause of the onlookers, dries his face within the hills and vales of her cotton blouse. Winking broadly at her audience, she climbs on her boyfriend's shoulders for a better view and says, "He's always been a lucky sort."

"Are they coming yet?" he asks.

"No, not yet. They're just now lowering the plank. How many do you think there'll be?"

"Four or five hundred, they say."

"Really? It's such a tiny ship."

"It sure is, but they're pretty small, and they pack them in tight."

"But honey, how come they're letting them in now, after all those years of only letting Europeans in?"

"They don't have much choice anymore. It's been what? A good twenty years since the slaves were freed, and by now they're mostly either dead or gone to live in the rain forest, leaving the plantations desperate for workers."

"Oh, I'm so excited to see them," says the girlfriend. "When I was a little girl my aunt told me that they had fangs at the corners of their mouths and tails to pick things up with!"

"Nonsense," replies the boyfriend. "I sailed Tokyo Bay as one of Admiral Perry's cabin boys, and I can tell you, Japanese do not got fangs and they do not got tails. But they do have sort of funny slanted eyes."

"Like the Chinese? I saw some pictures of them in school."

"Nope, not quite the same. Japanese eyes slant down, and Chinese eyes slant up. Or is it the other way around? I forget."

"Oh," exclaims the girlfriend, "here they come!"

Murmurs of excitement rise from the crowd as the immigrants, slowly emerging from the darkness of the ship's holds, squint against the equatorial sun and pierce the air with foreign calls as they bump around, searching for family and friends.

"So how do they look?" asks the boyfriend.

"Can't tell quite yet. They're out on the deck now, but they're mostly hidden by the stuff they're carrying. But oh . . . here we go! The gangplank's in place, and they're starting down it."

The immigrants move along the dock to the customs house, where they are stopped by officers standing before a closed gate. The officers take their passports and shout, *"Bala! Ter que dar bala!"* (Candy! You must give us candy!) over and over again.

Forewarned by traders before having left Nippon, the passengers understand the call, but to a one, they pretend not to. After years of drought and marginal harvests, few could afford to pay a meaningful bribe even if they were willing, having at most a few lengths of hidden gold chain with which to confront an uncertain future.

The disturbance continues, with the officers' demands netting only puzzled looks and upturned palms—some practiced so well as to merit acting awards—until finally, for one senior officer, frustration overwhelms greed, a gate is opened, and buckets of passports are set beyond it.

The passengers trickle through the opening and, after retrieving their passports, continue onto land. But here, once again, confusion reigns. Though the organizers of the trip had promised immigrants and employers alike that all immigrants would arrive with large photo ID tags, showing both their names and their designated employers, no such tags exist. So now, the plantation representatives, as well as the immigrants, shrug and wonder in equal puzzlement.

The confusion is gradually aborted by Akiro Miroka, a middle-aged Nipponese of elegant stance and fastidious grooming. Carrying aloft a small Nipponese flag, he matches—while striving to keep friends and families together—workers with representatives. And in that way, over hours, wagonloads of tired but happy immigrants leave the port to start new lives.

Though their working destinations will differ, the Nipponese immigrants will reside together as planned, in enclaves yet to be formed; thus lessening the shock of living and working in a foreign culture, while carefully preserving their own culture and coordinating their work.

They will work hard and save well, always looking forward to the day when, as once again financially responsible citizens, they will proudly return to their beloved Nippon to live happy lives as loyal subjects of His Divinity the Crane, Emperor Hirohito.

2

Victory!

Rio de Janeiro, August 15, 1945

Sirens, church bells, and horns and drums give chaotic quiver to the air as spotlight beams, slanting through the midnight sky, emblazon Christ the Redeemer as, from atop Mount Corcovado, He casts His blessings on the multitudes celebrating below.

Adding to the cacophony, megaphone trucks, shepherded by the movements of the masses, repeatedly blare: *"Attenção! Attenção! ... Grandes novidades! Hirohito submetter-se! A Segunda Guerra Mondial é terminado!"* (Attention! Attention! Great news! Hirohito has surrendered! World War Two is over!)

Celebrations continue through the night, but the news does not bring equal joy to all.

3

Loyalists and Defeatists

Countryside, State of São Paulo

1945

Near the bank of a stream, a score of Asian men, their features alternately shaded and illuminated by a flickering campfire, sit cross-legged on the ground. Before them stands a hooded man who says, in a strong young voice: "Then we are agreed. We will coordinate our harvests to increase our profits and hasten our return to the Land of the Rising Sun."

Agreement, riding on applause, fills the air.

Someone signals and, being immediately recognized by the speaker, says, "Then it is true, despite what the round-eyed devils say, that Nippon remains victorious."

"Yes, it is true," says the hooded man. "I heard it in the words of His Divinity, the Crane himself, over the radio of my patron. He praised our victorious sailors for sending the Allied Navy to the bottom of the Sea of Nippon."

"Then the *Brasileiros* simply lie to mask our victory," says another, "when they say His Divinity has surrendered."

"That is so," says the hooded man.

An outraged voice roars from the darkness. "But that lie is told not only by the Brasileiros. It is also told by some of us Nipponese! Right here in Brasil, even in our enclaves!"

"True," says the speaker. "There are such traitors. They are the Defeatists. Most are youngsters who have left our enclaves, some are adults

5

who no longer live among us, and a few are adults who live secretly among us and serve as spies for the Brasileiros."

"We must silence them. We must silence all the Defeatists, children and adults, lest they poison the minds of the others!" shouts another.

"Yes, we must!" aroused voices agree.

"But what of our older children gone away?" says a fragile, older man, "And what of those at Brasilian universities? Some speak like Brasileiros. Some, I have heard, even think they *are* Brasileiros."

"Such older children, by siding with the Defeatists, become one with them and must be treated the same as the others. No longer dutiful children and Loyalists, they can only be considered to be one with the adult Defeatists, who must be silenced by us," replies the speaker.

"But only by secret means," cautions another.

"Yes, of course. Anything we do must be kept secret from the Brasileiros, says the hooded speaker, or they will use our actions as excuses to enter and try to control our enclaves."

Murmurs of agreement give rise to the cry, "Silence the Defeatists!" The chant becomes ever angrier as it is repeated.

When relative quiet returns, the speaker says, "Again, we are agreed. We will silence the Defeatists. But to do so, we must have names. Go home and get names. But keep all names secret. If we tell the names, the Defeatists will tell the Brasileiros, who will try to silence us.

"Tomorrow morning, a stone box bearing a carving of a crane will appear in the entrance hall of the temple of the thunder god in Aruja. Leave the names for me, unaddressed and anonymously, in the box. The stone box will remain in place for only three days, so we must work in haste."

"And then?" asks a tall, older man.

"Then you will all be called to meet to make plans to destroy the Defeatists."

A hoarse voice cries out. "When? When? When will we meet? We must act soon!"

"You are right. We must act soon. Then, if all agree, let us meet here at the next full moon. Do all agree?"

All do.

"Good. But remember, we must always keep all things secret. That includes our own identities. And it would be well if those of you not already acquainted do not now recognize one another in public. A few of you have recognized me despite the hood I wear, but do not tell your neighbor who I am, and do not talk to me in public. We will operate best in total secrecy.

I shall wear my hair behind me in a braid, so that, when we meet at other times, you may know me by sight, if not by name, and may approach me if there is need."

The speaker lowers his hood, revealing a face masked by a dark lotion. As if they contain tiny beacons, his intense black eyes reflect and project the ember light of the dying fire. And his hair, long and darkly resplendent, trails behind him in a single long braid that reaches to his waist.

"And now," he says, "if none have urgent need to speak, let us depart for home."

All stand, and with whispered farewells and many bows, they leave— some by foot, some by donkey, and some by canoe. Only the hooded man remains, smiling with profound satisfaction. *Perfect,* he reflects. *Cooperation among us will hasten our return, and eliminating the Defeatists will ensure the purity of our community.*

Taking a bowl from his canoe, the speaker gathers water from the stream, douses the remaining embers, and turns his attention to the southern sky, where a great darkening, accompanied by thunder and lightning, is quickly shading the light of the sun.

Good. Heavy rain is coming this way. It will shift the sand and remove the signs of our meeting from the sight of all.

Departing in his canoe, the braided one paddles quickly toward the advancing darkness and soon passes beyond the clouds and rain, becoming but a dark silhouette traveling in a swift canoe. An observer sees him as a man flying a tattered flag from a canoe that skims across the moonlit water, but the flag he sees is not a flag at all. It is an abundance of long black hair that, released from its braid, tosses about, cooling the paddler with welcome gusts of nighttime air.

4

Meeting the Buddha Amida

1949

Akiro Miroka, white-haired and wan, lies mortally ill in the supervisor's quarters of *Cafezal Tres Lagos*—Three Lakes Coffee Plantation.

His daughter, Kaede, a college-age beauty of golden complexion, sits on his bed holding his hand—a fine hand, even in his advanced age—in her own elegant hands, while a doctor stands by.

The room is plain and plainly furnished. Its only opulence is a shrine featuring a golden statue of the Buddha Amida, precisely positioned to receive the day's first sunlight from the bedroom's eastern windows. Twice as tall as the head of a man, the statue is framed by a filigreed gold corona that glows in the light of the seven votive candles that burn before it. Beneath the porcelain table on which the Buddha sits is a splendid leather case, tooled and dyed with scarlet and white and violet flowers that sprout from intertwining vines that form windows to the living Paradise that is the Buddha Amida's home.

Akiro stirs from his faint of minutes before, shakes his head, and resumes the tale he had been whispering into Kaede's ear. "And so, with no other choice than suicide by seppuku, and barred from that choice by my duty to your mother, I left our beloved land with the truth unknown to any but my wife, my general, my emperor, and myself."

"Ah, Father, at last I understand why you left the land you love so much. But could you not have redeemed yourself by explaining to your general that it was your lieutenant's order, not yours, that caused the needless deaths of so many of the emperor's soldiers?"

"No, Kaede, no. What greater dishonor for a commander than to blame his dead lieutenant for a tragedy that occurred during the commander's watch!"

"But still, Father, your actions in the emperor's service were correct and pure. You had not yet been informed that the Russian division your lieutenant was attacking had offered to surrender. Your ill fortune was not in any way due to your own negligence. It was but the work of the demons of death, those monsters who live in the shadow universe surrounding ours, waiting, always waiting, to spread disaster when we go to war or otherwise attract their notice."

Akiro, slipping away again, does not hear these last words, but moans in such great anguish that Kaede steps back to make room for the doctor. He examines Akiro's eyes, listens to his fluttering heart, squints in anguish at what he hears; and then, pocketing his stethoscope, nods permission for Kaede to return to her father's side.

Akiro soon wakes again; confused at first, he slowly recognizes Kaede, who holds his hand to her heart.

"Oh, Father," she says, "thank you for telling me of the trials of your earlier life. I now understand why you have always said—unlike the parents of my friends, who insist that their children consider themselves Nipponese—that I should think of myself not as a displaced Nipponese, but as a new Brasilian, beginning her adult life in a country of great beauty and opportunities."

"Yes, such are the reasons for my insistence, my daughter. Though it grieves me greatly to realize that, following such a path, you will be deprived of the priceless joy of living in the glorious land of your ancestors, bathed by the breezes arising from the emperor's endless grace."

"Don't be aggrieved for my future, Father. With the many blessings you and Mother have bestowed on me, I shall find happiness wherever I am, treasuring my ancestors all the while. The esteem in which I will always hold them does not depend on where I live.

"But why, Father, why did you not speak to me of this before?"

"I could not, my daughter, I could not. Not while your mother was alive. And after her death, it somehow … somehow seemed too late. But it now comes to me that these are things you must know. It is not the knowledge of these things that can harm you, but the lack of it."

"You couldn't tell me while Mother was alive? I don't understand."

"I was afraid you would blame me, as I have blamed myself, for her death. How shamed by me she must have been to take her own life, while still so young and innocent!"

"No, Father, no! It was not so. Mother spoke to me, child though I was, of the many times the demons of death came to visit her, urging her to join them. It was they, not you, who drove her to act as she did."

Akiro, his eyes widening in astonishment, says, "If only I could be sure! If only I could be sure!"

"You can be sure, Father, you can. Many were the times that Mother told me how honored she was to be your wife, just as I am honored now and forever to be your daughter."

Akiro smiles vaguely as he drifts toward unconsciousness; and then, gathering his strength in an effort that shakes his feeble frame, he fixes his gaze on Kaede. Pointing a shaking finger at the statue of the Buddha Amida, he says in a breaking voice, "When I go, Kaede, take the Buddha Amida with you and guard him well. He was a gift from the Emperor Meiji to my father. A gift given in recognition of your grandfather's leading the emperor's armies to victory in the first Chinese war.

"Take the Buddha Amida and keep him safely with you, Kaede, for it is he who will give you the freedom and the means to be of help to your fellow Brasilians.

"Just as it has been my duty, as a loyal subject of His Divinity, to serve my fellow Nipponese, so it is your duty now to serve your fellow citizens here in Brasil."

"I understand, Father, and I will do as you say when it is time. But it is not yet time."

"Yes. It is time, my daughter, it is time. Look! Look there! There at the horizon. See how the earth and sky are splitting apart? They split to form a passage for my entry into the *bardo*." (transitional state between death and rebirth.)

Kaede lifts her father's hands to either side of her face and cries, "Father, no! Father, don't leave me! Not now. Not now. My need for you is so great."

But Akiro, his face a mask of otherness bearing a statue's expressionless eyes, emits an eerie wail and dies.

The doctor, moving quickly, searches first for a pulse and then for a pupillary reflex. He holds a mirror before Akiro's nose and mouth and, a minute later, withdraws the mirror, shaking his head in sad negation.

Kaede kisses her father's sweat-dampened brow and opens the door to a tiny porch, where senhor Pedroso Salles, the owner of Cafezal Tres Lagos, and a group of workers wait. With a motion of her hand, she invites them to enter.

Senhor Salles, a well-dressed, handsome man of middle age, who would look even younger than he does, were it not for patches of white in his sideburns, joins Kaede at her father's bed, where he lays a hand on her shoulder and whispers words of condolence. But Kaede, overtaken by grief, hears him not, for her head has fallen to her father's chest, where she cries with abandon.

Senhor Salles withdraws and is replaced by a worker, Masaru, a tall, young Nipponese who, intensely dark of eye and hair, is an imposing presence, even in such a mournful situation. He is the son of senhor Salles's deceased gardener who, killed at an early age by a venomous snake, left Masaru to be raised—under senhor Salles's willing patronage—as Kaede's principal childhood companion.

Masaru whispers regrets to Kaede as he squeezes her hand, and though she does not speak, she lovingly returns his squeeze. Masaru then takes Akiro's rice bowl from his night table and, bowing all the while, backs from the room. On the porch, he signals the other workers to enter.

The workers approach the bed, one after the other, speaking brief condolences, followed by bowing retreats from the room.

Finally, only Kaede and the doctor remain. After carefully closing Akiro's eyes—though once closed already, they had slowly reopened—the doctor slips from the room, leaving Kaede to her grief.

The sun has set and darkness is descending when Kaede, by the faint light of dying candles, kisses her father's cooling brow and covers his body with a sheet. She kneels at his bedside a few moments longer, then rises and faces the Buddha Amida. She lifts the Buddha from his shrine but, unprepared for his weight, lets him slip from her grip. He drops onto the porcelain table, cracks the surface of the table and slides backward, a fall from which Kaede barely manages to catch him.

She lifts the Buddha again, this time wrapping both arms around him and lifting him to her chest. Having a good grip on him now, she slowly lowers him into his case and straps the case shut. She loops the straps over her shoulder, snuffs out the single candle still burning, and carries the Buddha from the room.

The following morning finds Kaede in her bedroom, sitting in the lotus position. Before her, standing on a table made of a single piece of the beautiful maroon heartwood of the Jacarandá da Bahia tree, is the Buddha Amida, fronted by a garden of offerings of ginger and flowers, and a seashell filled with water. Light from a crescent of candles illuminates both the Buddha and Kaede, who was up at dawn to gather the fresh, pure water for the Buddha's seashell. The water came from a spring recently sprouted from the earth, which Kaede's father considered a gift sent to him by the Hindu God Vishnu, the supporter of life, to whom he had long been devoted.

Kaede wears an exquisite silver kimono. At her neck, a ring of pale golden dogwood blossoms intertwine on an indigo collar, sending off vines that sprout a splendor of jewels to twinkle along the rest of the robe. The kimono, along with the Buddha Amida, constitutes the whole of the physical universe to which Kaede attaches value. The one was her mother's deathbed gift; the other, that of her father.

Kaede raises her joined hands to her crown and, pausing in that position, says, "Once more, dear Buddha Amida: With mind"—she lowers her hands to her mouth and pauses again—"with speech"—and lowering her hands to her heart—"and with heart, I take refuge in your compassionate embrace.

"And I beseech thee, oh Buddha Amida, to hasten my father's passage through the bardo, and, releasing him from further reincarnations, let him join his fellow Buddhas in the Pure Land of Peace and Provision and Supreme Fruition.

"To this end, though I am certain that my father, compassionate being that he is, has many times earned the merit required, I offer all the merit I may have accrued during this and all my previous lives."

She chants: "Namo Amida Butsu, Namo Amida Butsu, Namo Amida Butsu," affirming her gratitude to the Buddha Amida for favors rendered her father. As she chants, the Buddha metamorphoses from a small statue to a greater-than-life-size figure, who floats high before her in the air, smiling grandly, his arms extended in welcome. In a resonant voice that originates from everywhere at once, he says,

Your father, Kaede, after delaying his passage through many reincarnations in order to return to earth to help others on the path, has finally consented to enter the Realm of the Pure Land, where he now and forever resides, in

the company of his fellow Buddhas and in the Perfect Peace he has so fully earned.

With those words spoken, the Buddha Amida crosses his arms over his chest and disappears into the dark of Kaede's swoon.

On awaking, Kaede, drawn by an irresistible compulsion, moves close to the statue of the Buddha Amida. Kneeling before it, she studies its every detail closely, until finally, her attention is fixed on a small flake of gilt that curls away from the surface of the Buddha's skirt. She frowns. *How odd! It looks like the slightest touch would cause it to fall away from the wood beneath it, but it remains, even after I so clumsily buffeted the Buddha about in moving him. In any case, I must repair it. Or better, I will ask Masaru to repair it. I could carefully lift it off now to prevent further damage, and give it to Masaru to seal back in place. That way, the piece won't be lost.*

Kaede polishes her nails against the inner hem of her kimono and examines them closely. Finding them clean, she gently lifts an edge of the flake with the nail of her index finger. She expects to expose a bit of wooden surface, but instead discovers what seems to be a second layer of gilt beneath the first.

Strange. Gilt on gilt? Why would anyone …?

Her curiosity thoroughly aroused, she turns the statue over on her lap. *Oho! I almost dropped it. It's so heavy.*

She examines the statue's base. It shows a few indentations, but no separation of gilt from the underlying wood.

The indentations look like the normal effects of many moves, but it's still strange that no gilt has separated from the base. I wonder …

She scores the statue's base lightly with a prong of the jade and silver ring, a gift from a close friend, that she always wears. The groove that forms is smooth and round, lacking the wrinkles she expected to see. She scores the groove again, harder this time.

The groove, though deeper and wider than before, neither wrinkles nor cracks as she expected it would.

The groove is so smooth and even. How? Oh, could it be? "Could it be!" she says aloud.

Wildly excited now, she presses the prong of the ring against a single spot in the center of the groove. A smooth and perfectly symmetrical indentation, with just a tiny hole through the outer gilt layer, results. And at the base of the hole …

"It's gold!" she exclaims. "Solid gold!" *They covered the gold with gilt to disguise it. To make is seem but another beautifully carved wooden, gilt-covered statue.*

After carefully returning the Buddha to his shrine, Kaede again sits before him, her hands pressed together in prayer, her fingertips against her chin. Looking upward, she says, "Thank you, dear Father, for giving me the means to be of help to others. I did not understand before, but now I do. I shall always and only employ the Buddha to promote the ends you desire."

Slipping back into meditation, Kaede is resting in boundless space when a sharp knocking at her door brings her back, though a bit confused at first. She waits, and the sound is repeated, more loudly than before, but in a rhythm that is most familiar.

She rises, walks to the door, and opens it to Masaru. Her father's rice bowl, broken in half, is cradled in his hands. He bows and, looking past her into her room, sees the candles burning before the Buddha and says, "Ah, you are praying to the Buddha Amida. So sorry to disturb you."

"No need to apologize, Masaru. You did not know."

"I will not stay. I came but to give you this." He shows her the pieces of her father's bowl.

"So thoughtful of you, Masaru, to break my father's bowl. Now his hungry ghost will have to go elsewhere for the rice it seeks."

"I did not want it to bother you."

"Thank you."

"It is only a small favor to render the daughter of your honorable father. But now I must go. Will I see you tomorrow? I will be repairing the roof of my cabin in the morning, but will be free by midday."

"Yes, tomorrow. Let's meet after midday," says Kaede as, accepting the broken bowl, she lightly caresses the backs of Masaru's hands. "I'll be here, at Tres Lagos, all day."

"I will find you," says Masaru. He bows, turns, and strides off at his usual rapid pace, his long dark hair, carefully arranged for visiting Kaede, flowing like a flag behind him.

Kaede smiles as she watches him disappear among the trees.

A few days later, Kaede and dona Elsa are sitting on a bench near the Japanese garden that Masaru has created and continues, a bit each day, to create for senhor Salles. The women are watching Gétulio, senhor Salles's son, play stick and hoop. The garden, Kaede reflects, for perhaps the hundredth time, is lovely. *A true work of art and devotion. One that only a truly centered spirit could create in his calmest moments.*

At the garden's center is a large koi pond, formed by man and nature combined. Over many years, a creek originating in distant hills has constantly channeled rainfall down to a great wall of stone birthed by the early earth. The creek, so long deflected into a curve, has carved the earth beneath it into a bowl-shaped pond from which the creek's overflow leaves the pond by way of surmounting a series of upright copper plates installed by Masaru—plates which emit musical notes as the water flows over them on its way to feed the fields below. The number and volume of the notes, established by years of experiment, is dependent on the volume of the overflow, which varies with the season. Today, it being early in the dry season, Kaede counts five notes—a clear melody at a discreet volume.

How brilliant of Masaru to create constantly changing, always pleasing concerts.

At the center of the pond a little island, connected to land by an arched wooden bridge, supports a small pagoda housing a teakwood Kuan Yin, Buddhist Goddess of Mercy, before whom Masaru and Kaede often sit and meditate. Senhor Salles acquired the statue on a trip to Rio, and presented it to Masaru as a reward when he completed the pagoda.

The bridge to the island is the continuation of a trail bordered by beds of sculpted sand and stone that Kaede, Masaru, and—as recent footsteps suggest—even senhor Salles use for walking meditation.

The entire assemblage—pond, island, bridge, trails, and garden—is the product of Masaru's labors. His father gave him many useful suggestions, and senhor Salles offered to assign helpers to him, but Masaru turned down all offers of manual assistance and insisted on building the project entirely on his own. Starting in his late teens, it took him nearly three years to complete the basic plan.

The first year he spent gathering stones from the fields to create the island. He carried the stones to the pond by wheelbarrow, ferried them by skiff to the island site, and one by one dropped them in place. The island slowly emerged from the water.

The second year, Masaru assembled and shaped wood from the forest to build the pagoda and the bridge. Also that year, he asked his father how he might get a statue of a Buddha to place in the pagoda. Masaru's father, who knew of senhor Salles' planned surprise, only answered Masaru with smiles and inscrutable comments like: "Just build the pagoda, Masaru, and if a Buddha finds it good enough for a home, he will move in on his own."

With the pagoda finished by the end of the second year, the Buddha Kuan Yin did move in, and Masaru spent most of the third year concentrating on the garden—collecting and planting special flora bordering the sculpted trails leading to the bridge. Since then, the garden has continued to be Masaru's ongoing project, receiving his attention nearly every day.

*

"What a pretty blue dress you're wearing, dona Elsa," Kaede says. "The color goes right to your eyes, making them even bluer than their natural hue."

"Thank you, Kaede. At first I hated wearing the same color every day, but it does make it easy to dress, and both senhor Salles and Gétulio say it makes it easier to find me."

Her brow suddenly wrinkling in concern, dona Elsa stands and calls out, "Gétulio, that's far enough. See if you can roll the hoop back to us."

Kaede and dona Elsa chat about small things for a while until, in the distance, they see senhor Salles leave the casa da cafezal with an arm around a pretty young blonde in a tight red dress. He walks her to the driveway, where his chauffeur holds open the passenger door of a Bentley.

Taking the woman by the hand, senhor Salles helps her into the car. As soon as she is seated, she glances at her hands, raises her eyebrows in delight, and says, her luscious lips moving with extravagant mobility, "Thank you so much, senhor, I always adore the time I spend with you."

"Paulo," says senhor Salles, "please take the dona to the bridge, wait until she has boarded her bus, and then come right back for me."

"*Sim*, senhor," Paulo replies as he salutes.

Senhor Salles waves good-bye as the car drives away, and is blown a two-fingered kiss in return.

*

Masaru is on his knees, trimming a small Seiju elm in the Japanese garden, when the sound of footsteps on volcanic pebbles causes him to look up. "Good day, senhor Salles."

"And a good day it is, Masaru, a true beauty of a day. One perfectly made to display the glory of your garden."

"Thank you, senhor." Masaru stands and wipes his hands against his pants. "Is there anything I can do for the senhor?"

"Well yes, Masaru. If you will forgive my interrupting your work, I would speak with you of an important matter."

"Senhor?"

"As you know, the death of senhor Miroka leaves me with neither a manager for the affairs of the estate, nor a supervisor for the workers of the fields, both of which functions he so ably performed. And though, for the present, I am content to manage the estate myself, I would like someone else to supervise the workers. And finally, since I know that the workers respect you and enjoy working under your direction, I would like for you to become their supervisor."

"The senhor trusts me so?"

"Of course I trust you, Masaru. I have known you and your work for many years. I can remember your father having you hard at work, day after day, when you were but a child, even though I sometimes wondered if we should let you spend more time at school in Aruja. Still, I marveled then at how well you followed your father's instructions, and I marvel now at how well you give instructions to others."

"I will be happy to supervise the workers, senhor. And I would say that the senhor should not regret my education. What I missed by not attending school in Aruja, I learned twice over from the tutors you hired to teach me over the years."

Well yes, senhor Salles thinks, *the tutors certainly did good work in teaching you to think and speak. But I wish you had had more opportunity to benefit from the socialization of community schooling. You are so alone.*

"I am glad you feel that way about your education, Masaru, and I'm also delighted to hear that you are willing to become supervisor. Now the only thing remaining is for us to speak of your compensation. In keeping with the greater demands of your new position, I propose to double your current salary. Does that seem sufficient?"

"Too sufficient, senhor."

"I'm glad you think so, Masaru. Then we are agreed?"

"Sim, senhor. The senhor is most generous."

"Good. And, oh, there is one more thing. Since the demands of supervision are many, I think you should surrender at least some of your gardening duties to someone else. Since you know the workers better than I, I would like for you to select that person for me."

"That will not be needed, senhor. I am sure that I can manage to both garden and supervise."

"Very well then. Let us experiment in that way, but do not hesitate to ask for help if you should find you need it."

"Sim, senhor."

Senhor Salles extends a hand to Masaru, who displays his dirty palms in protest. But the senhor, ignoring the objection, takes Masaru's hand in his and shakes it heartily, saying, "Today, Masaru, is not the first day that these hands have embraced the soil of this land."

*

A sunrise breeze spices the air with the scent of coffee blooms as dona Elsa, Kaede, and Gétulio leave the casa da cafezal. They are bound for a grove of trees near Lago Grande, where a surprise ninth-birthday present—designed by Masaru, and built by him and Kaede—awaits Gétulio.

"A swing, a swing!" Gétulio shouts as they approach a tall oak from which there hangs a swing. He runs to the swing, jumps onto its wooden seat and, standing tall, yells, "Swing me! Swing me!"

Dona Elsa swings him for a while, wanting him to get the feel of the swing before she lets him go it alone. She swings him higher and higher until, coming nearly level with the horizon, he brushes up against a knotted rope that hangs from a tree before him.

Returning to his point of origin, he points to the tree with the rope and shrieks, "Dona Elsa, there's a rope on that tree, and it's full of knots! And I see another rope hanging from a tree farther out!"

Dona Elsa holds the swing while she explains that Masaru designed Gétulio's birthday present so that when the swing reaches the rope on the second tree, Gétulio can catch it and use it to swing to a third tree, where another rope hangs before a platform. But, she emphasizes, reaching the platform will come much later, after he has practiced grabbing the first rope long enough to be sure of his moves. Until she tells him that he looks ready, he must practice just going back and forth on the first tree's swing.

"Oh, I see the platform," says Gétulio. "It is far away! But when I get there, how will I get back?"

There are two ways, Elsa explains. One, which he should use at first, is to stay on the platform and enjoy the view and rest. Then, when he's all rested, he can climb down the stick ladder on the tree trunk to the ground, and walk back from there.

Later, after a lot of practice, he'll be able to hit the platform with his feet, then kick off and return to the swing and the first tree using the same ropes he used to get to the platform.

"You mean use the extra ropes to swing all the way to the platform and back without stopping?" he asks, the thrill of anticipation illuminating his face. "I can do that!"

"Not yet, you can't. Not until *we agree* you are ready. For now, you shouldn't try to do more than just swing back and forth on this swing until I say you've practiced enough. But once you've practiced enough, it'll be easy. It took me, oh, about ten hours to get ready."

"Push me, push me!" he shouts. "I'm ready to practice!"

Dona Elsa and Kaede take turns pushing Gétulio, until he says, "You can let me go now. I'm ready to swing by myself."

Convinced that Gétulio is in good control of the swing, and getting tired of pushing him, the women retreat to a nearby bench to watch. From there they hear a stentorian voice, its owner hidden by trees, approaching from the direction of the casa. "Happy birthday, dear Gétulio!" the voice repeats until senhor Salles appears. He softens his voice and sings out, "Good morning, everyone."

"Good morning, senhor," the women reply.

"Good morning, *Papai*," Gétulio shouts. "Push me high and watch me swing!"

Senhor Salles pushes Gétulio higher and higher, until he touches the first rope. He springs from the swing and grabs on. Then, after swinging to and fro a number of times, building momentum, he grabs the second rope. Swinging on, he arrives at the third rope and the platform, which he bounces off of and returns to the seated swing on the oak where he slides down the rope and seats himself on the swing, humming in smugness, pretending not to be exhausted.

Truly astonished, senhor Salles—who didn't really know what the birthday gift would be, other than "a swing in the woods," runs up to Gétulio, plucks him from his swing and hugs him to his chest. He then dances around, shouting, "Everyone, look! Here is Gétulio. Just nine years old, and already becoming a famous acrobat. Bravo Gétulio! Acrobatic champion-to-be of the state of São Paulo."

A panting senhor Salles soon surrenders Gétulio to dona Elsa, who, recovering from the fear that possessed her when she first realized what

Gétulio was up to, sits the boy on her lap. They rest together for a while, both of them spent—the one emotionally, and the other physically.

Now senhor Salles, his breathing returned to normal, smiles at Kaede and offers her his arm. Accepting the offer, she places her hand on his forearm, and he leads her down the path. Walking at a leisurely pace, they climb to a hilltop where the path splits into trails leading to each of the plantation's three lakes. Senhor Salles chooses the path that leads to Lago Grande, where they walk to the end of the dock and sit on a bench facing the water.

They are quiet at first, both enraptured by the scene—by the beauty of the blooming trees and the clear blue sky, dotted with little white clouds—and by the copy of that view, reflected in a darker, abstract rendering by the surface of the lake.

Eventually, senhor Salles breaks the silence by asking Kaede a question, but hordes of cicadas, clamoring for sex in the surrounding fields, force him to repeat with a raised voice. "Kaede, I have accepted the chancellor's invitation to the Universidade of Sao Paulo's convocation, and am wondering whether you plan to attend as well."

"Oh, yes, certainly, senhor. I only left when I did because of my father's illness. But I do want to receive my degree along with my classmates. Also, as *valedictoriana*, I've been asked to give a little speech on behalf of my class."

"You are the valedictoriana! Congratulations! It has been so long since I spoke with you of your studies, that I did not know. That's marvelous."

Kaede, color coming to her cheeks, whispers thanks.

"In that case," senhor Salles continues, "let me rephrase my question. May I invite the illustrious valedictoriana to ride with me to the universidade? I plan to leave here a day early to visit with friends and will return directly after the ceremony."

"Thank you, senhor. I'd be delighted to ride with you—at least in going there. And going early will allow me to visit with friends as well. But I won't be able to come back with you, since other responsibilities will keep me there for a while. But, yes, it would be great to ride with you. We've had so few chances to talk of late."

"Fine. And would it be convenient for you to leave directly after breakfast? Let us say, about eight?"

"That sounds perfect, senhor."

"Excellent. This is working out exactly as I had hoped. And also, just by way of provoking your interest Kaede, I will confide in you now that, once on our journey, I will make you an important proposition."

"A proposition, senhor? Oh, tell me! I love propositions."

"Ah no, not yet. This one is a secret proposition, which I will divulge only once we are en route."

5

Unknown Visitors

Smoke billows from behind a distant hill as a teenage boy runs toward the casa da cafezal yelling, *"Fogo! Fogo!" (Fire! Fire!)*

Senhor Salles rushes from the house, sees the smoke, and shouts: "What's burning, Janio?"

"Kyoami's *casinha*, senhor."

Senhor Salles calls out twice for Masaru, but hears no response.

"Janio! Go find Masaru and tell him to bring my horse and the donkey cart—with a fire extinguisher. Immediately!"

"Where is senhor Masaru?"

"I don't know. Look in the barn first, then by the Japanese garden, and then by the lakes."

Janio races off, but soon comes running back. "I not find senhor Masaru. Cart not in barn, and donkey not in field. And I not see senhor Masaru in garden or from Lago Grande hill."

"Then saddle my stallion and bring him to me at once!"

Janio delivers the horse minutes later and senhor Salles leaps on and rides off at a gallop. He soon arrives at the few cleared acres where Kyoami's cabin had stood that morning. But instead of the cabin, he finds only smoldering embers, curled metal, and the ashen remains of household objects.

Circling the ruins, senhor Salles notices a number of hoof marks, most large and a few small, slowly filling with water seeping in from the boggy soil. The small marks are paralleled on both sides by narrow wheel tracks. *Three horses with riders, and the hoof marks and wheel tracks of a donkey pulling a cart.*

22

Moving away from the smoke and heat, senhor Salles sees a shadowy figure in the midst of a grove of trees. He approaches with caution at first, and then, realizing who is making the shadow, he hurries over to Kyoami's grandmother. Blind, shriveled, and bent by age, she is sitting on a stool, wrapped in a black shawl, emitting feeble moans.

Speaking in the calmest voice he can muster, senhor Salles says, "Do not be frightened, Little Mother, it is only I, senhor Salles. Are you all right?"

"Maaa, all right."

"What happened?"

"Men and horses come. Take me from casinha and put me here. Then I smell petrol and feel heat and smoke. Men laugh and talk, then leave. Is still much heat. Did casinha burn?"

"Yes. The casinha is gone."

"Things in casinha burn?"

"Yes, but do not worry, Little Mother. We will find you another casinha, and we will replace your things."

"Não replace things. Things too old."

"You say the men spoke, Little Mother."

"Maaa, men speak. One say, 'This teach Defeatists.' What be Defeatists?"

"Defeatists are Nippo-Brasileiros who believe the Allies have won the war, and … well, perhaps you should ask Kyoami about the Defeatists. Where is Kyoami?"

"Kyoami at market. He sell tomatoes."

"And the voice you heard, the one who spoke of the Defeatists, Little Mother. Did you recognize that voice? Do you know who it was that spoke?"

After a lengthy pause, she says, "Não. Não. Never hear before. Never."

"Was the voice that of a young man or an old one?"

"Was young man. But não hear before. Não. Não hear before."

"Did you recognize *any* voice?"

"Não, não recognize any."

"When will Kyoami return?"

"I feel sun be low, so Kyoami soon return. He always return before sun go sleep."

"Do you want to come to my casa to wait for him?"

"Maaa, não. I stay here. Kyoami find me."

"All right. But tell him to come see me as soon as he returns. If I don't see him by nightfall, I will send someone for you."

"I tell. And I pray the *Santa Virgem* bless you, senhor."

"And many blessings to you, Little Mother. I am leaving now, but do not be afraid. Janio will bring you water and food, and will stay with you until Kyoami returns."

"I não afraid."

*

Senhor Salles is sitting in his great chair, watching a pair of deer feed on sprouting shrubs just outside a window, when Kyoami, escorted by dona Elsa, appears at the library door.

"Come in, Kyoami. Come in and sit down," says senhor Salles, indicating a chair near his own.

Kyoami, too winded to speak at first, points to his dirty work pants and remains standing.

"Kyoami," says senhor Salles, "how is your grandmother?"

"She is upset, senhor, but she not hurt."

"Good, I'm glad to hear that she's not hurt. But now, I need your help. Your grandmother told me that the men who burned your casinha said they were doing it to teach a lesson to the Defeatists. Who were these men? Do you know them? Are they members of the Loyalists? And why would they choose your casinha to burn?"

"I believe they be Loyalists, senhor, but I not know who they be." He pauses, searching for answers, then says, "Maybe they burn casinha because they think I be Defeatist."

"Are you?"

"No, Senhor. I honor my ancestors and my emperor, so I not Defeatist. And I be Nipponese who not want to be Brasileiro, so also not Defeatist."

"Then why do they think you are?"

"I not know, senhor."

"Tell me, do you believe that Nippon has lost the war and that Emperor Hirohito has surrendered?"

"Yes, I believe so, senhor."

"And do you state those beliefs in public?"

"I believe Allies win war, but I never say in public. I only tell my brother and priest that I believe. But they não tell others. Não, they never tell others. Maybe Loyalists think I be Defeatist because I não go to Loyalists meeting at last full moon. I invited to meeting, but I não go."

"All right. But still, we must find out who burned your casinha."

"I not know who, but my grandmother know. She know voice of leader. She almost tell me, then she become afraid and não tell."

"But she told me she did not recognize any voices."

"She não tell you whose voice, senhor, and she não tell me whose voice, for she be afraid. But she know. I know she know. When I ask if she know, she wait long time before say she not know. That is how I know she know. To lie is hard for her, so she always wait long time before she lie. But later, when she not so afraid, she will tell me, and I will tell senhor."

"Yes, you must tell me just as soon as you know. Above all, we must maintain peace and safety for everyone at Cafezal Tres Lagos."

"Sim, senhor. I tell senhor as soon as know."

"Good. And now, let us talk about housing for you and your grandmother. You could move into the old casinha in the north field. It is smaller than yours, and its roof needs thatch, but perhaps it will serve until yours can be rebuilt."

"I thank senhor. I know casinha in north field. It serve good."

"Fine. Let dona Elsa know when you are ready, and she will give you some of the household things you will need. Also, I have spoken to Masaru. He has agreed to help you move, and will also take charge of rebuilding your casinha. In the meantime, watch your grandmother carefully, and tell me at once if you think she may need a doctor."

"Yes, senhor, I watch her careful. I thank senhor from heart. Senhor be most holy patron."

*

Days later, Masaru, coming from a barn with a donkey cart full of tools and materials, encounters senhor Salles in front of the casa da cafezal.

"Good morning, Masaru," senhor Salles says. "What is the state of Kyoami's casinha?"

"Almost finished, senhor."

"So quickly?"

"Sim, senhor. Planting for the season is finished, so many workers are free to help."

"Excellent. And the arsonists, the ones who set the fire? Any word on their identities?"

"Não, senhor. I've asked many, but so far, no one tells. All say that they must be Loyalists and that some in Aruja must know their names, so I will keep asking."

"Yes, please do that, Masaru. Kyoami says his grandmother recognized the voice of their leader. He also says she is afraid to name him now, but that she will do so when she is less fearful. So be sure to question Kyoami frequently, just in case he hears but hesitates to tell me."

"Ah, senhora Kyoami can hear! She never speaks, so I thought she did not hear."

"Yes, many think she's deaf because she rarely speaks. Perhaps she does not like to speak because she cannot see who is listening, but in any case, both her hearing and her speech are intact."

Masaru nods. "I will keep asking. Kyoami will tell me when he knows."

"Good. I appreciate your efforts, Masaru."

6

A Love Revisited

Kaede sits cross-legged on the ground at the edge of the woods, not far from the casa da cafezal. Her mind is drifting with the breeze, transported by the beauty of the golden haze that blankets the field before her, when senhor Salles's Bentley quietly approaches.

She does not hear the car at first, and senhor Salles, charmed by the bliss of her expression, motions for his chauffeur to cut the engine. He watches Kaede for a few minutes, until, growing uncomfortable with what feels like spying, he has the chauffeur start the car again.

The polite starting sounds reach Kaede. She turns, smiles, waves, and strides off to the casa. Going directly to her bedroom, she exits minutes later with a suitcase, which is taken from her by the chauffeur, who has been waiting at the casa's front door. As he carries the suitcase to the car, Kaede re-enters the casa. She emerges moments later with the Buddha Amida strapped in his case and riding on her hip. At the car, she passes the Buddha to senhor Salles, and joins him in the rear passenger seat.

As the chauffeur starts to drive away, senhor Salles tells him that he has heard, via shortwave, that the main road to São Paulo has been cut off by a mudslide.

"*Não é problema*," the driver replies. He will use an alternate route, he explains, which though longer, is on the dry side of the mountain.

Senor Salles closes the privacy window between the front and rear compartments of the car and turns to Kaede. "Kaede, I would like to further inquire of your plans following graduation. You already informed me that you will not be able to return to the cafezal with me because of other commitments, but I would still like to know—if it's a prediction you can make—approximately *when* you will return."

"I can't really say, senhor. All I can say for sure is that it will, at the latest, be shortly after the elections, though it may well be much sooner than that. In any case, I mean to return as soon as I can. Tres Lagos always feels like home to me, so I'm always eager to return. Most of all to be with you and Gétulio and dona Elsa, but now also to further explore my relationship with Masaru, who has spoken to me with serious intent."

"Good. I'm pleased that you want to return as soon as possible. And I'm glad that you consider the cafezal to be your home. It surely is your home, just as much as it is mine."

"Thank you, senhor, it's sweet of you to say that."

They ride in silence for a while, thrilling to their passage through a section of road covered by a floral tunnel of braided greenery, strikingly perforated, here and there, by sparkling beams of sunlight. But on exiting the tunnel, they approach a scene of roiling violence that brings the car to a sudden halt.

Where a path crosses the road, two bullocks, so alike they might be twins, circle and rumble and charge, inflicting bloody wounds on each other. The whole encounter, it appears, is simply a show for the amusement of the young *gaucho* who, standing in his stirrups, cheers them on.

"Oh, they're bleeding," says Kaede, reaching for the door handle. "We must stop them."

"Stay inside," says senhor Salles, arresting her hand. "It's too dangerous out there." He cranks his window down and shouts, "E´, gaucho! How long do you think it will take senhor Mendoza to throw you out into the street once he hears how you care for his cattle?"

"Excuse me, senhor, please excuse me. I was only being inattentive for a moment. It will never happen again. I promise. Never again!" The gaucho quickly separates the bullocks, then salutes senhor Salles.

"It had *better* never happen again!" shouts senhor Salles, motioning for his driver to go on.

"I shall still inform senhor Mendosa," he tells Kaede. "Though I didn't want to tell the gaucho that. It would be too easy for him to eliminate the evidence by running the bullocks over a cliff."

Calm returns as they progress down the road, and senhor Salles turns to Kaede and says, "Please tell me if I am being too inquisitive, Kaede, but you just spoke of Masaru expressing 'serious intent' in regard to yourself. I take it that means he wants your hand in marriage. But tell me, if you will, whether you share his 'serious intent.'"

"Your understanding is correct, senhor," says Kaede. "He has asked for my hand, but I've been unable to respond either one way or the other.

"As you know, we were very close as children, right up until I left for the universidade, but it's been almost five years since, with only a few short visits in between. And now I'm just confused. Sometimes I'm sure I love him just as much as ever, and at other times he seems like a total stranger. So clearly, I need both time and proximity to rediscover Masaru—as well as myself—and to determine whether we, who related so well as children, can continue to relate as adults.

"His wish is to marry me and return to Nippon, while I want to be a part of the new Brasil. That alone should tell me what I need to know, and yet … and yet … I continue to desire the joy we once shared—the joy we both have so long dreamed of recapturing."

Senhor Salles nods and goes back to watching the beautiful flora passing by.

*

Kaede closes her eyes and revisits a scene from the past. In that scene, she and Masaru, both seventeen, sit on a horse cart at the intersection of the Caminho Real and the road to the cafezal. They are holding hands, their eyes locked together, and are about to embrace again, when they hear a motor laboring uphill.

"That must be the omnibus," says Kaede.

And shortly, a silver bus with São Paulo Centro on its front marquee and Transito Rapida painted on its side, stops nearby. It squats, rises, drops back down, and finally opens its doors with a pneumatic sigh that seems a comment on the steepness of the hill.

Masaru and Kaede share another long and tender kiss, and Kaede takes one of Masaru's hands from her waist and cups it over a breast. They stay that way until, in a voice rendered nearly inaudible by emotion, Masaru says, "It is so hard to let you go, Kaede. We were so close last night."

"Yes, Masaru, yes. It is the same for me. It's almost impossible for me to leave. And yet I must. If I miss this bus, I will miss registration, and maybe lose my scholarship."

"Last night was the first time I touched all of a girl."

"And it was my first time touching all of a boy."

"It was wonderful!"

"It was wonderful for me too, Masaru. But now I have to go."

"But before you leave, please tell me, why did you not let me enter your veiled place?"

"I couldn't. I don't know why not. Maybe it was because I was about to go away. But later you will enter there, Masaru. I promise. I will guard it for you. But last night I couldn't."

"You will guard it for me . . . and *only* for me."

"Yes, Masaru, *only* for you."

"Promise?"

"I promise."

"Kaede?"

"Yes?"

The bus driver lightly taps his horn.

"Masaru, I must go."

"Go. I will think only of your return."

"And I'll constantly dream of returning to you."

She kisses Masaru again—on the mouth, on both cheeks, and on both hands.

The bus driver, charmed but running late, gets off the bus, takes Kaede's suitcase from the road, and shelves it. She follows the driver, and the bus moves off, slowly at first, with Masaru running alongside waving, until the bus gradually gathers speed and pulls away, leaving Masaru standing in the road, becoming smaller and smaller and smaller.

Kaede, returning from her voyage to the past, notes the bemused expression on senhor Salles's face. "I'm sorry, senhor. Was I gone for long?"

"No, just a few minutes. But it was interesting to watch your expressions."

"Which were?"

"Expressions of love. Of love and innocence and anticipation. I haven't seen such an expression of innocent love in years, not since I lost Bertha. Sometimes I provoked such expressions from her, though more often it was Gétulio."

Senhor Salles seems to Kaede to be on the verge of crying. She takes his hand and clasps it warmly between both of hers, until, some minutes later, he gently slips his hand away and says, "Thank you, Kaede. You are sweet."

Kaede waits until, convinced by his expression that senhor Salles's strongest pangs of sadness have receded, and says, "Senhor, you spoke of a proposition you would put to me during this trip. I can't wait to hear it."

"Yes, yes. I was just searching for the words to state it. In fact, it was in regard to that proposition that I asked you earlier when you planned to return to the cafezal. Briefly put, I would like to enlist your services as Gétulio's tutor and advisor."

"But you already have dona Elsa."

"Yes, and dona Elsa is an excellent governess, whom I hope and intend to keep. But now that Gétulio has reached the age of reason, I would like for him to be tutored by someone of greater education, someone more aware of the rapidly changing post-slavery culture of Brasil. After all, he will one day become the patrono of the cafezal, inheriting all the responsibilities that such a position presents."

"I am touched by your offer, senhor Salles. Touched and honored, but I don't think I can accept it. You see, though I intend to return to Tres Lagos as soon as I can, I may have to leave again anytime—to serve as a government functionary."

"As an appointed functionary?"

"Yes. If the PDP's senatorial candidate is elected, I've already been told that I will be asked to be his main advisor and spokeswoman. It would be a chance to serve my country that I could not decline."

"And the PDP is?"

"Oh, I'm sorry! I should have said *Partida Democratica Popular*. It's a political party that's been around for years, though it's not very well known because its members are mostly students. Also, the party has been illegal ever since it was founded in '39, though it's been tolerated because it's been politically powerless. But now, with the war over, many people who are tired of autocracy are crying out to choose their own government, and a lot of them are turning to the PDP.

"All of a sudden, lots of people, even a few of the power elite whom you may know, want to join us in our efforts to create a popular democracy if, as rumor has it, we are soon to be legitimized."

"And you're concerned that becoming Gétulio's tutor might interfere with your political duties?"

"Well, yes, there's that, and vice versa as well. I'm also concerned that my political activities might deprive Gétulio of his tutor's presence when he needs it most."

"I see. But I think I also see a way to accommodate both your needs and Gétulio's. What if I assigned dona Elsa to be your assistant? In that way, you could come and go as necessary, leaving her to maintain continuity for Gétulio in your absence."

"We could try that," Kaede says thoughtfully. "Dona Elsa and I do work well together. But I wonder if she would feel slighted."

"She won't, not if I give her a large raise at the same time that I appoint you."

"Aha. She does like money, so that should work."

"Then you accept?"

"Oh, yes, senhor. I've always wanted to be a teacher. And it's such rare good luck for a new graduate to be hired right away to do what she loves, with people she loves."

"Excellent. Then there remains only the question of salary."

"I don't want money from you, senhor. You have been so kind and generous to both my father and me for so long, it seems almost, well, like it would be avaricious to accept pay for working with Gétulio, whom I love like a little brother."

"Bless you, Kaede, for your loving generosity. But you are about to be a graduate, and as a graduate, you should be compensated at a level reflecting your qualifications. However, if you prefer, I will decide the amount of your compensation myself, provided you promise to tell me if it seems insufficient. Agreed?"

"Agreed."

7

A Graduation Surprise

Arriving for convocation, Kaede and Roberto and some friends, enter the *amphitheatro* of the Universidade of São Paulo. Their destination is the section, facing the speaker's podium, traditionally reserved for graduating students. But they all stop just inside the entrance, thrilling to the view before them. The limestone amphitheatro, a good likeness of a pre-Christian structure still extant on the Isle of Kronos, glows a luscious orange in the early evening sun.

"It's so timelessly beautiful," Kaede says.

"Yes," a friend replies. "It does look timelessly beautiful, and timelessly wise as well."

"It must also be the home of a poetic muse," adds Roberto. "Witness the way you two illiterates unravel metaphors before you even sit down."

As they take their places on benches with their classmates, Kaede and Roberto join the others in joking about their approaching "moment of glory" (Kaede's phrase), and the lot of them snuggle ever closer together. Several friends, too curious to wait, try to get Kaede, who is starting to feel a bit of speaker's anxiety, to reveal the topic of her valedictory message. All they get in response are skyward glances and feigned grins.

Only a little past the designated hour, heraldic horns announce the official procession; and the graduates' rippling pond of humorous wishes and affections for one another gradually quiets. The procession, moving at a stately pace, follows the chancellor and the marshal at arms across the field, up the stairs, and onto the stage.

At the marshal's direction, the faculty is seated mid-stage on several limestone benches, and the five honored guests are seated in imitation Louis XIV chairs on a platform above and just behind the faculty.

33

The chancellor welcomes the audience and the faculty and guests, all of whom receive a standing applause from the others.

"Thank you for your warm reception," says the chancellor as the applause dies down. "And now, let us begin."

Extending an arm in the direction of the guests, he says, "It is both my honor and privilege to begin the introductions with our illustrious guests, all of whom—as important supporters of the mission of the Universidade— generously advance the well-being, not only of our students, but of all of the people of the *Estados Unidos do Brasil.*"

Stepping close to the guests, the chancellor opens a hand to the nearest of them and says, "First, please recognize His Excellency, senhor Fernando Quadros, *Governador do Estado do São Paulo,* whose administration supports our mission in many ways."

The governor stands to considerable applause.

"And next, please welcome Colonel Emilio da Costa Brava, *Commandante das Policias Estadual,* whose efforts as commander of the state police help maintain the peace that reflective education requires."

Polite applause greets the colonel.

"Continuing," the chancellor says, as he touches the next guest's shoulder, "it is a special privilege to present to you senhor Pedroso Salles, who endows our largest senior scholarship fund. It is a much sought after scholarship, which is awarded to the three most academically distinguished students in each year's class. It is simply called *Bolsa para os Meritoriosos* (Scholarship for the Meritorious) because, such is senhor Salles's humility, he would not permit us to name it in his honor as we wished to do."

Senhor Salles smiles and nods in thanks during the explosive student applause that follows.

"And here," the chancellor continues, bowing lightly to a man in plantation whites, "is a man whose name, if not visage, all will surely recognize. He is the illustrious senhor Carlos Pinheiro, director of the Coffee Producer's Society, whose distinguished family has provided Brasil with no less than three *presidentes.*"

Strong applause, mostly from older guests, follows as senhor Pinheiro, his chest covered with medals, waves to all, while projecting a pleasant, though distinguished air, of a type much practiced by the remnants of the country's once official royalty.

Next the chancellor—using the rounded end of his staff—gently nudges an ancient prelate who, his chin firmly shelved on his chest, dozes away in scarlet garb. As the prelate awakens, the chancellor says, "Finally, let me present His Eminent Holiness, Cardinal Capybara, who adds the spiritual blessings of the one true church to our temporal efforts in higher education."

The cardinal, eyes half open, blesses the audience with an abbreviated sign of the cross and promptly goes back to sleep.

As relative quiet returns to the amphitheater, a group of men, all wearing similar gray suits, reclaim their seats but continue to scan the audience, some with the naked eye and a few—mostly concealed by posters or shadows of the walls—with binoculars.

"And now," the chancellor says, "with our primary introductions accomplished, let us turn our attention to those we are here to celebrate: the new baccalaureates!"

After a loud and lengthy applause, the chancellor continues, "Though young, their youth but increases the greatness of their promise. They, and others like them, give us new sources of light and hope as, at the conclusion of a great war, we seek a path to lasting peace. And now, let us hear from the graduates themselves, beginning with the introduction of the valedictoriano, who will, per tradition, address us on behalf of his class."

A growing murmur, full of giggling, rises from the student section and sends the chancellor to his notes. He finds his mistake at once, but, forgetting that his microphone is on, whispers to the marshal at arms, "It's a first—a triple first! A woman, a Japanese, and a valedictoriana, all in one."

Wild laughter from the student section brings a blush to the chancellor's cheeks, but he quickly recovers and says, "Correcting my error, for which I sincerely apologize, let us welcome the most academically distinguished student of her class, dona Kaede Miroka!"

Kaede walks onstage to strong applause, punctuated by a few wolf howls from male students, and receives her diploma from the chancellor. He shakes her hand while congratulating her, adjusts the tassel on her cap to the graduate position, then steps aside to give her access to the lectern and its microphone.

Kaede bows, first to those onstage and then toward the audience in each of the sections of the amphitheatre. She waits, glowing self-consciously, for the applause to diminish, then says, "Thank you. Thank you all.

"First, on behalf of my class, I wish to express our gratitude to all the kind and generous individuals, some known and some unknown to us, who show their love for their country by helping students everywhere. Your efforts will be rewarded by the always vigilant Spirits of Good, who will add happiness to your lives in the form of blessings unanticipated.

"Next, as valedictoriana, I must share with you the fact that I was surprised when I first heard that I had been chosen for such an honor. Was there a clerical error? I wondered. I knew then as I know now that there are others in my class equally or more deserving. But, once assured that my selection was not an error, I ran to find a dictionary. I needed to know—if I was to become one—what exactly was a valedictoriana. What did the word mean? Was it good or bad or neutral?"

Over light laughter, Kaede goes on. "Perhaps because the word begins with a *v*, I thought it might mean something like *the victorious one*. But no, to my ego's chagrin, I found that *vale,* the beginning of the word valedictoriana, has at least two archaic meanings. One, derived from the Latin *vallis* is 'valley,' while the other, derived from the Latin *valere*, means 'be well,' as when we say *fare-thee-well* when someone is leaving.

"Continuing my search, I next discovered that the latter part of the word, *dictoriana,* did not, as my ever-vigilant ego had secretly hoped, mean that I was fit to be dictator. Rather, it meant it was up to me to provide the diction—the words—to wish you the blessings of the gods for my class."

Cardinal Capybara opens his eyes at the word *gods*. He listens for a moment, and then, convinced that he is not being called upon, goes back to sleep.

Kaede continues. "Also, in the form of a *valediction*—in this case, the saying of farewell—I want to urge you all to say farewell to our current form of government. Though perhaps warranted in the past, it is now, with the conclusion of the Second World War, time for us Brasilians to say fare-thee-well to government by fiat of the privileged, and welcome to government 'Of the people, by the people, and for the people,' as was so elegantly said by Mr. Abraham Lincoln of the United States of America."

A riotous tangle of agreement, questioning, and outrage rises from the audience.

After out-waiting the loudest rumbling, Kaede says, "Acting in pursuit of the establishment of a truly democratic government, it is now my privilege to introduce to those of you who do not know him, my leader and fellow graduate, winner of the Scholarship for the Meritorious, and chairman of the Partida Democratica Popular, Roberto Millefiore! Senhor Millefiore, please stand and be seen."

Kaede points toward Roberto, who stands and salutes the persons on the stage and the audience. At his salute, a pre-arranged signal, a number of students uncover hidden horns and drums and line up in ranks. They begin playing martial music that is in the spirit, if not exactly according to the rhythms, of a John Phillip Sousa march. The music, in turn, sends a group of students from the stands to the bowl of the amphitheater, where they unfurl and display a huge banner that reads: *PDP! Liberdade, Igualdade, e Fraternidade Para Todas! PDP!* (PDP! Liberty, Equality, and Fraternity for all! PDP!)

Waving her arms in encouragement, Kaede chants the slogan at the audience, from which a chorus, rapidly growing in number, chants it back, over and over again.

Meanwhile, the chancellor, somewhat disconcerted by the totally unexpected political activity—which he secretly admires—is unsure how to proceed. He studies the guests on stage.

Governador Quadros is frowning, but unable to imagine that any student movement might be significant, looks more puzzled than upset. *Probablemente não problema.*

Senhor Salles is smiling in bemusement. *Não problema.*

Cardinal Capybara is still sleeping soundly. *Não problema.*

Senhor Pinhiero, though clearly surprised, doesn't seem at all upset. *Não problema.*

Colonel Costa Brava, scowling and frowning, is clearly agitated. *Problema!*

Catching the chancellor's gaze, the colonel snarls at him. "This is an outrage, Chancellor! They, an illegal party to begin with, are using a state function to carry out an insurrectionist demonstration! Is *this* what you call education?"

The chancellor and the marshal at arms purse their lips and look away.

The colonel jerks around, facing Senhor Pinhiero. "And you, senhor, you are from Rio. Tell us, are such speeches permitted at O Universidade do Rio?"

"Similar things have happened in Rio," senhor Pinhiero responds. "They happen in Rio, and they happen elsewhere from time to time. But, Colonel, such things are not important. Student movements come and go, and in Brasil, the greater the demand for change, the less change actually occurs. Surely you know this as well as I."

Still red of face and scowling, the colonel turns to Senhor Salles. "Senhor, I am told that this one, the valedictoriana, is from the Japanese enclave at Aruja, which is near your cafezal."

"At one time," senhor Salles replies, "she was of Aruja, but she now resides at Cafezal Tres Lagos."

The colonel's expression clouds. *Careful, careful! Senhor Salles has powerful connections.* In a lowered voice, he says, "The senhor will please forgive me if my curiosity seems excessive, but it is, of course, my duty to monitor all elements of emergent political movements. May I respectfully ask in what capacity the valedictoriana shares your domicile? Is she a member of your household staff?"

"I consider her, Colonel, a member of my family."

"Aha! Very good, senhor. Now I understand. And please allow me, as a fellow male, to congratulate you. She is a rare beauty indeed, and as we all know, politics are irrelevant in the bedroom."

Senhor Salles, curling a lip in disgust, turns his back to the colonel.

Kaede, meanwhile, diploma in hand and unaware of the drama taking place on the stage, joins Roberto at the head of his parade. With banners stretched across the three columns they have formed, the participants, totaling several hundred now, march and dance and skip around, shouting and singing the PDP's slogan. As they complete their third tour around the bowl, Roberto turns to face the marchers and raises his hands, a signal that sends the demonstrators hurrying back to their seats.

Kaede returns to the podium, picks up the microphone, and says, "And now, on behalf of my class and celebrating the honor of your attention, I say to all of you, and to all our fellow Brasilians, fare-thee-well, and may many blessings be yours as you venture through the vales of life."

Taking advantage of the relative silence of the largely still astonished audience, the chancellor takes the microphone from Kaede and says, "Thank you, Miss Miroka, for a most stimulating address.

"And now, let us recognize the *salutatoriano* of his class, senhor Sebastião de Guanabara!"

A robed student climbs to the stage.

*

Early evening finds Kaede and Masaru walking slowly along the path leading to the Japanese garden. They are holding hands, though loosely. He is waiting for her to speak, and she is searching for the words.

How can I say that I love him, which is true, while at the same time tell him that I may come to him and yet may not? I might as well just say that I'm too crazy to accept or reject his proposal—which isn't far from the truth.

Kaede had asked for the walk, saying she had to talk to Masaru about their relationship. She knows he is eager to hear what she has to say, and that he fervently hopes she will say that she is going to be his.

As they follow the trail onto the bridge that spans the koi pond and leads to the pagoda, a vortex of wind suddenly spins leaves and seeds and floral debris into a column that briefly surrounds them. The vortex passes on, but the clear blue sky grows dark and menacing, and unleashes a panorama of thunder and lightning followed by great sheets of cold rain. They run to take shelter in the pagoda. The darkest clouds and the rain soon pass on, but strong winds remain.

"Look," says Kaede, pointing a shivering finger out the pagoda's single heart-shaped window. "The spirits of good weather are turning the prayer wheels. Listen carefully and you can hear their mantra: *Go storm demons, go! Go storm demons, go!*"

"Yes," says Masaru, "I hear them. The spirits of good weather that ride the wind have come to chase the clouds away."

When the wind dies down and the sun returns to the sky, Masaru and Kaede leave the pagoda and resume their walk. Following the downward course of the stream exiting the pond, they arrive at a spot where the stream widens. On the other side, a trio of alligators sun themselves on the bank.

With Kaede still silent and Masaru growing increasingly anxious, they sit on the bank, simply listening to the gentle sounds of the moving water. Gliding in from the sky, a great blue heron crashes into the water, rights itself, and begins to prowl the creek in search of food. It prances forward, stopping after each measured step to stand upon a single leg, tilt its head, and carefully search the water below. Prance-tilt, prance-tilt, it repeats but then, suddenly jerked downward by an unseen force, it squawks, flaps its wings against the water, and disappears.

The remaining pair of alligators do not move, but continue basking on the shore, while feathers from their companion's feast float downstream.

Though reminding herself that nature's way is nature's way, Kaede can't help feeling sorry for the bird. Not wanting to see what other products of violence might rise from the water, she lies back. Closing her eyes against the sun, she tries again to find the words to speak compassionately, while delivering what must be, for both of them, an unsatisfactory message.

Just as she is about to speak, Masaru springs upon her, draws her to him, and, holding her tightly, kisses her passionately. Startled, Kaede struggles to free herself, but Masaru is too strong, and she soon quits the struggle. Then, to both his surprise and hers, she joins him in his ardor, as rushes of desire overwhelm her initial resistance. But then, with them mouth on mouth and stroking each other's bodies, Masaru abruptly grasps a breast so painfully that Kaede shoves him away with a strength she didn't know she had.

"Why do you push me away?" he demands in a husky stranger's voice as he sits up. "You promised."

"I promised?"

"You promised to be mine. Only mine!"

"Masaru, that was years ago. That was the promise of a *child*, and I'm a woman now."

"And you no longer want to be mine," he growls.

"I didn't say that. The truth is that I would like to be yours, but we have been apart for so long that, before I can be yours, I need to know much more about the spirits that drive your love . . . and about those that drive my love for you as well.

"For most of our lives we grew up together, leading constantly interwoven lives. But now, with all the years that have passed, we meet again as adults who barely know each other. Part of me still loves you and yearns for the love we once had. But until we find out who we both have become, I can't give myself to you or to any other."

"Aha! And *who* is any other?"

"There is no *any other*. I was but expressing a thought."

"You lie! You do have another, and it is because of him that you will not come back to me. You belong to only him."

"No. I belong to no one, Masaru."

"You do. And I know who he is. He is Roberto!"

"No!"

"Yes! I have heard about you and Roberto. I have been told by those who know. And it is for Roberto that you deceive me, and also want to dishonor your ancestors and become a Brasileira. All of that I know!"

"Well yes, you are partly right, Masaru. There *is* a Roberto. He is the leader of the party I serve as secretary. But he is *not* my lover, and I *do not* belong to him. He is my leader and my friend and that is all. Though," she adds, "it is true that I have thought I might one day welcome him as my lover—just as it is true that I might one day welcome you as my lover.

"But, Masaru, right now I don't know to whom I should go. And if you want to give me a chance to get to know you once again—which I must do if I am to join you—you must understand that it is love and tenderness that will speak to me, *not force* and *not demand!*"

Masaru stands and walks away, along the edge of the creek. *What can I do, what can I do?* he wonders. *She works for a Defeatist. No, he is not a Defeatist, he is an Italo-Brasileiro. But it is because of him that she acts like a Defeatist. So what can I do? What can I do to take her away from him? What can I do to bring her back?*

Ah, I see. First I must separate them. And then, when she returns to Tres Lagos—and senhor Salles says she has promised that she always will—then I will be kind and gentle, and I will take her to be mine, and she will love me and I will make her understand that she is still a Nipponese and we will return to Nippon and raise beautiful, loyal Nipponese children.

After crossing a bridge to the other side of the creek, Masaru sits, facing away from Kaede but still in her view, and assumes the lotus position.

Kaede is greatly relieved to see Masaru sit. *Ah, he calms himself. Driven as he is, he's still able to calm himself—a trait that may give us a chance. It's so wonderful that the spirits of good befriended his mother and showed her the path. He'd be dead from his temper by now if his mother hadn't, again and again, over all those childhood years, trained him to meditate. And how he used to hate to do it as a child. He used to run and hide, sometimes in my secret hiding places. But his mother never gave up, and she won. So now he uses meditation to calm himself. Bravo, Masaru! And may the gods continue to bless you and your mother!*

Kaede waits a long while, hoping Masaru will return to her in an approachable mood but, emotionally exhausted and feeling mired in confusion, she soon gives up and heads for the casa da cafezal.

Later, while hanging her sheets from her balcony to air them in the sun, Kaede sees Gétulio approaching on the path below, dragging a pair of paddles. He shouts, "Dona Kaede! Dona Kaede! I want to go canoeing! I want to go canoeing with you!"

"And canoeing we will go," she sings back, delighted to share his cheer. She joins him, and together they head for Lago Grande, creating a song as they walk:

"Canoeing we will go,
Canoeing we will go,
We will paddle in the sun,
And on the lake, have good fun!"

8

Deliverance

Senhor Salles, as long has been his habit, accepts the Sunday paper from his chauffeur and retires to his library where steaming *cafezinho*—a small cup of strong coffee—and warm croissants await him. He lifts his cafezinho from its saucer on a blue marble table, takes a tiny sip, adds more sugar, and sips again.

Smiling in satisfaction, he puts down his coffee and opens the paper, the Brasilian edition of ***The Herald International***, to the front page and reads:

The Rising Tide

Sunday, October 12, 1949—In the city of São Paulo and in other major cities, rallies organized by the Partida Democratica Popular (PDP) have, of recent days, been drawing ever-larger crowds. An estimated 70,000 persons gathered Monday at the *Praça da Republica* in São Paulo and, according to the organizers, "easily" 50,000 gathered at Copacabana Beach on Thursday!

With only a few minor exceptions, the rallies have been peaceful, consisting mainly of music, dancing, picnicking, and drinking. A good party, only occasionally interrupted by speeches and a few "other disturbances."

The police, though maintaining a watchful presence, have—surprise of surprises—behaved with restraint, despite the fact that the PDP remains an illegal party at this time.

43

Can it be that "the powers that be" have come to understand the urgency of the people's wish for representative government?

Let us hope so, for it is time. The many are agreed:
It Is Time!

Even as Senhor Salles reads, Roberto, flanked by assistants, finishes a speech at the Praça Amada Prada in Curitiba.

"And so I call on you, all of you, to join with the PDP as have the transit workers and the stevedore's unions, in a general strike beginning tomorrow at midnight. We shall be heard!"

He raises his arms in a victory V, and the crowd, cued by onstage assistants, begins chanting, "PDP! Liberdade, Igualdade, e Fraternidade Para Todos! PDP!"

Roberto leads as banner bearers and a band start the crowd down the path that circles the praça's periphery. Almost at once, three large canvas-covered trucks, led by an unmarked van with mirrored windows, converge on the praça. Soldiers with bayonets leap from the trucks, surround Roberto and his associates, and separate them from the others.

A captain of the state police, moving as if he were taking a casual stroll, descends from the van and asks who is in charge.

"I am," says Roberto.

"And who are you, young senhor? Kindly let me see your social identity card."

The captain reads the card, emits a low whistle, and says in a mocking tone,

"Senhor Roberto himself! The colonel will be impressed.

"And your permits, if you please. I must see your permits. Two are required. One for the construction of a stage on public property, and one for the formation of this assembly. Surely you have the required permits."

"I have no permits," Roberto says. "I tried to obtain them, but they were refused on the grounds that the PDP is an illegal party."

"Then, my dear young man, you are obviously in violation of not just two, but at least three laws, and I must place you under arrest."

The captain signals one of the policemen, who promptly handcuffs Roberto, arms behind his back.

Picking up a megaphone, the captain next addresses the crowd: "You are all to disperse at once, or you will be arrested. I repeat: you are all to disperse at once, or you will be arrested."

He turns to the policeman guarding Roberto. "*Sargento*, take this man and lock him in the cage in the van. We will take him to a location where he will get the treatment he deserves. Then have your men check the social identity cards of all the others of the group onstage. Let those whose cards are in order go free, arrest the remainder, and confiscate the public address equipment and the musical instruments. Also, call demolition and have them remove the stage."

His orders given, the capitão and his driver, lights flashing and siren blaring, take Roberto away, leaving the soldiers and policemen to their work. Amid a rising stew of murmurs and shouted insults, the crowd, pressed backward by a human fence of slowly advancing bayonets, moves in the only direction left open and slowly pours from the praça.

*

Roberto, after a day and a night and a day of questioning by the police, is transferred by boat to a prison, long reserved for political dissidents, on an island a few kilometers off the coast of Rio de Janeiro.

He arrives after dark, his personal effects and clothing are taken from him, and he is issued a long, smelly gray shirt and a pair of oversized straw sandals. Along with its seven current residents, he is locked into a cell designed for two. He spends the night crouching in a corner—the only uncontested space in the cell. Its four tattered hammocks are occupied, and the rest of the floor already claimed.

In the morning, after a breakfast of acrid coffee and moldy bread, Roberto and half of the building's other prisoners are turned loose in the debris-littered prison yard. The boundaries of the yard are established on three sides by tall concrete walls, spiked with broken glass and surmounted by coils of barbed wire. The fourth side of the yard, established by the prison building itself, presents the viewer with a sight most bizarre as hundreds of arms and faces, framed by narrow windows created by the omission of alternating concrete blocks, move and shout and stare in an animated collage.

At the center of the yard stands a tower capped by a roofed platform from which four machine guns, one for each quadrant, protrude. The tower provides its gunners with a clear overview of the men who mill around in a guard-driven circle, bumping into one another, sometimes unavoidably and sometimes intentionally. Fights frequently erupt because of the bumping, and for many other reasons too.

Roberto, sore of joint and somewhat crazed by sleep deprivation on this, his first "daily promenade," as the guards call it, sees imaginary fireflies flickering on and off, despite the daytime light. Exhausted as he is, he can barely walk at all, but the crowd keeps him in motion until, only minutes into the forced walk, dark clouds send slanted rain whipping down on them.

The angle of the rain allows one concrete wall to provide shelter for those who arrive in time to huddle along its length. But there is not enough room for all, so many are left to choose between risking a fight trying to wrestle their way in, or shivering in the frigid downpour.

Roberto chooses not to run for the wall. Instead, he stands where he is, near the center of the yard, and strips off his clothes. He is using the rain, cold as it is, to clean his clothes and self, when someone bumps him from behind.

He turns to find a small young man, the name Candido inked on his forehead. His crudely bandaged hands hang limp, leaving him to use his elbows to try to fit a large plastic sheet over his head and torso.

"*Por favor,*" Candido says, holding his hands out front.

"*Certo,*" Roberto replies, as he wraps the frayed plastic around Candido and ties its ends in a knot above his shoulders.

"*Grazie.*"

"You're welcome," Roberto replies in Italian. "But shouldn't you try to go inside—or maybe try to get to that wall?"

Candido lifts a hand in the direction of the guard tower. "No, the wall is too crowded now, and we must not try to go inside, not before the afternoon rain is done. If we do, they will shoot in our path as we approach the door. It's a little game they like to play with newcomers—a little game that sometimes kills."

"I see," says Roberto. "But what happened to your hands?"

"The guards broke them."

"Why?"

"I'm not sure. They kept spitting on me and yelling '*Comunista*' while they hammered on them."

"Are you a Communist?"

"No. But I don't speak Portuguese, and I don't have a social identity card. I think they were just guessing, or maybe just amusing themselves, by creating a reason for sending me here."

"Why don't you have a card?"

"I didn't know I needed one. I just arrived a few weeks ago as cargo in a box of hams from Sicily. I was to meet a cousin in Rio de Janeiro who said he would have all the papers I would need, but I was arrested on the street before I could find him."

Roberto and Candido pace silently in a little circle of their own until the rain stops. Then someone blows a whistle, and a phalanx of guards, clubs in hand, drive the inmates from the yard, squeezing them, with the help of many jabs and blows, through the smaller of two doors that lead back into the prison.

Someone slips a note into Roberto's hand as he is rushed down a hall and minutes later, back in his cell, he reads:

> *Dearest Roberto,*
>
> *Colonel Costa Brava ordered your arrest, but senhor*
> *Salles has since spoken with Marechal General Janio*
> *Cruzado, who has promised to arrange your release,*
> *along with that of your associates. However, the Marechal*
> *said your release will take a few days, and he said I should*
> *advise you to be "most careful" in the meantime, so as not*
> *to give your captors any excuse to harm you.*
> *You will soon be free, for the spirits of good are with us.*
>
> *Loving you,*

Kaede

Roberto smiles in relief and settles back into his little corner, which is where, despite a growing pain at the base of his spine, he will spend most of the rest of the day and night.

*

Just after dawn, Roberto and his cellmates wake to a tumult of shouting and screaming. A guard bangs a club against the bars of their cell, opens the door, and yells, "Get out! Get out! The prison is on fire! Run to the dock!"

More shouting and banging echoes from many parts of the prison as Roberto and the others rush for the yard. On the way, Roberto pauses for

47

a moment to stare into a locked cell, where the shattered face of a guard squirts diminishing arcs of blood onto his chest and the rifle that lies across it.

As the men surge into the yard, the gates of the prison swing open and the prisoners, hunching beneath bursts of machine gun fire, fired high to hurry them on, dash from the prison and down the road that leads to the dock.

Within minutes, with the prison nearly empty, the gates clang shut. Nothing more is heard from the prison until some minutes later, when a few more bursts of machine gun fire are heard, after which silence returns.

"What was that last shooting about?" Roberto asks the man running alongside him.

"Probably putting an end to the cripples, poor bastards," says the man. "Them and anyone the guards owed for drugs or women or other favors."

At the dock, troops herd the prisoners onto a large ship, and within minutes a cheer goes up as the ship, sounding its whistle to the accompaniment of shouts of glee, steams away. A party soon develops, with singing and dancing and drinking, and the rumor quickly spreads that the drinks have been provided by Marechal General Janio Cruzado.

Someone produces a radio, and many gather around to hear that the army, now under the command of the Marechal, has disarmed the presidential guard and dissolved the government, sending the president and his cohorts into Bolivian exile. Further, the announcer practically sings out in delight, "The Marechal has ordered the immediate release of all political prisoners!"

Cheers abound aboard the ship, briefly drowning out the radio announcer. With the return of relative quiet, the listeners hear that the Marechal has decreed that the country will temporarily be governed by a transitional council consisting of himself, the Chefe dos Policias Federales, the Chefe do Departamento d'Enterior, and the Almirante Commandante da Marinha—the Admiral in command of the navy.

"The council," the announcer continues, "is taking as its first mission, the specification of a date on which general elections will be held to form a truly representative government. One based solely on the popular vote. And that democratically elected government will, at the earliest possible date, replace the transitional council as the government of the land."

Later dispatches announce that all adult Brasilians will be required to vote in the coming elections, and that all political parties, including the previously illegal Partidos Comunista and Democratica Popular, have been legitimized by the council. They, and all other political parties, are encouraged to help the Brasilian people, especially those isolated in the interior, to access voting places to help create a government that truly reflects the wishes of *all* of the people, urban and rural, rich and poor alike.

Near sunset, the ship docks at O Porto do Rio, and the passengers, some carried by others, walk down the road that, seven kilometers later, will bring them to the city of Rio de Janeiro.

Roberto and Candido are met at the dock by Kaede, who leads them to senhor Salles's Bentley, a break for which they both are most grateful, given their physical condition.

Roberto sits in the driver's seat. He wants to drive for the sense of freedom that self-determined motion promises, but maneuvering to leave the parking lot, he realizes that he is much too weary to be trusted, and passes the wheel to Kaede.

It is late already when Kaede drops Candido off at the home he shares with some other party workers, and later yet when Roberto and Kaede find their way to his apartment. It is so late, and Roberto is so tired, that he actually asks that his nocturnal temptations with Kaede be delayed until morning, in favor of his getting some much needed rest on the sofa, while she sleeps in the bed. It is a request that Kaede wistfully, but with understanding, agrees to.

After breakfast and bed, and despite the urgency of his political duties, Roberto drives Kaede back to the Cafezal, where he meets with senhor Salles over coffee, while Kaede searches for Masaru.

Better that Masaru and Roberto at least meet each other, she reasons, *if for no other reason than to make it harder for Masaru to imagine Roberto as a horned demon, or whatever image might come to his mind.*

But though she searched all the likely locations, she did not find Masaru before she and Roberto had to drive to the Camino Real to catch the morning omnibus to São Paulo. So Roberto and Masaru remained strangers, even though Roberto's visit, from start to finish, was closely watched.

A few weeks later, Kaede and senhor Salles, having finished an excellent dinner of wild turkey, manioc, and okra, take their cafézinho at a table on the edge of the koi pond—the better to the watch the comings and goings of a migration of saddle beak storks temporarily nesting in nearby trees. The table is positioned not far from the cafezal's library, the doors to which they left open, the better to hear the shortwave broadcasts of pre-election activities. This evening, the broadcasts are unusually clear.

Senhor Salles asks Kaede whether she has had any word from Roberto, and even as she shakes her head in negation, they hear:

"Meanwhile, political rallies held by no fewer than seven independent parties have taken place throughout the country. In Rio, São Paulo, Recife, and Belo Horizonte, to name just some of the larger cities, crowds the likes of which this reporter has never seen except at Carnaval, are gathered together to dance and drink and sing the praises of a form of government they have never known!

"Yesterday, at the beach at Salvador da Bahia, I came upon a trio of beautiful Bahianas dressed in glittering floss, who led a crowd in a dance to the rhythm of African drums.

"Why are you dancing? I asked."

" 'For the dance itself,' one said."

" 'Yes, for the dance itself,' echoed a companion, 'but also for *democracia* and the of return some of the riches of Brasil to the purses of the people. To people like us, the real Brasileiras and Brasileiros, who work and work but never earn, for all is taken from us by those who have no need.'

"And with those words, the Bahiana gyrated away, swaying in rapture. Ah, how I wished I were a young Bahiano just then!

"This is Carlos Santana for *Radio Unico*, saying: Viva Brasil Democratica!"

Masaru is in his garden restoring a finely raked geometric pattern in the sand, one rendered chaotic by a sextet of three-horned chameleons. He captured them all, and they now are resting in a fine silk net awaiting translocation to a less formal place. It is a hard move for him to make, since he finds them so beautiful he wants to keep them in sight; but maintaining perfection in his garden leaves him no other choice. He will take them to an area with the sort of lush vegetation that attracts the insects they love to eat.

It's not too far away, and the vegetation there changes color with the seasons. I will be able to visit them at different times and see how well they mimic their different surroundings.

As Masaru rakes, Kaede approaches. They exchange slightly formal bows, and Kaede asks, "May I sit?"

"Certo," replies Masaru, excited by a ray of hope.

He carefully props his rake against a rock and, indicating a bench that overlooks the garden, leads Kaede there. They sit, and Kaede gently takes his hands in hers and says, "Masaru, I have come to tell you that I must soon leave for São Paulo."

"For São Paulo? When? For how long?"

"I'll leave tomorrow by the morning bus, but I don't know for how long. That will depend on my party's needs. It might be for just a few days this time, with more visits soon to come, or it might be for as long as the entire two months until elections. I'm not sure. It depends on too many things."

"Ah, 'too many things.' I know the meaning of 'too many things.' 'Too many things' means the arms of Roberto!"

"Oh, stop it, Masaru. I'm *not* going to Sao Paulo for the arms of Roberto. I'm simply doing my job as secretary of the PDP. Though of course I'll be seeing Roberto. I've already told you he's our party's candidate for senator."

"And me? And us? You have no duty to us? Can't you stay here to help us find each other again, as you suggested and as I agreed—so that we may one day return to the land of the Crane?"

"Masaru, Masaru! Of course I have a duty to us, but that does not mean I haven't other duties as well. Many people depend on the promises implicit in my acceptance of the position of secretary of the PDP."

He barks, "I do not want you to go. I want you to stay. I command you to stay!"

"Don't shout at me, Masaru. I have given my word, and I must go. And it's time you understood what I've already told you. You may *not* command me. *Not now or ever!*"

Masaru's face darkens with anger, partly toward Kaede, but also toward himself as he realizes how badly he has handled the current encounter. Feeling driven to act, but unable to decide how, he jumps up and kicks his rake. It skitters across the sand, destroying much of his careful design.

Though frowning, Kaede speaks in a gentle voice, "Masaru, the time for isolation and dreaming of a life continuous with that of our ancestors is over. The empire and its emperor no longer exist. All of that and the other traditions you venerate, either have been or are about to be officially terminated.

"The Defeatists are correct in their belief that Nippon has been defeated. The emperor has surrendered to the Allies and has renounced his divinity, and the *Norte Americanos* are writing a new constitution for the Nipponese, which will formally end the empire. These are all known facts.

"And besides, here in Brasil is where we make our livings; and here, most likely, is where we will live and die. So it follows that we should think of ourselves as Brasileiros and Brasileiras—or Nippo-Brasileiros and Nippo-Brasileiras, if you like that title better."

"Lies!" he shouts. "All lies. Defeatist lies. The emperor has not surrendered, and he has not denounced his divinity. You betray your emperor! You betray your ancestors! Go ahead and be a Brasileira. Go, and do not return."

Turning his back to Kaede, Masaru grabs his rake and viciously claws at the ground as Kaede runs off in tears.

*

Early the next morning, Kaede adds the final piece of clothing to the suitcase on her bed and tries to close it by hand. She can't, so she sits on it and latches it shut. Next, she turns to the Buddha Amida's shrine and bows low. She places him in his silk-lined case, then slips the golden cobra heads of the case's twin belts through their silver buckles and fastens them. That done, she is sitting on her bed, mentally reviewing the things she's packed and wondering if anything has been forgotten, when she is startled by a staccato knock at her door.

Oh, no, she thinks in alarm. *I don't want to answer that. Not now. In an hour, I'll be rid of him. At least for a while.*

"Kaede, open the door!" a voice demands.

That settles it. I'm not here.

Minutes pass. She waits.

But here come new words, gently spoken this time. "Please open the door, Kaede."

She continues sitting.

"Please, Kaede, please," pleads a childlike voice.

Trembling, she opens the door, bows briefly as a distancing formality, and stands aside so Masaru may enter.

Once in the room, he falls to his knees and says, "I beg you to forgive me, Kaede. When last we spoke, you came in kindness, and I responded in anger. I did not mean what I said. I was only speaking from fear—from fear of losing you."

"I know," says Kaede. "I know."

"I beg you to forgive," he says again. He stands and walks past her to her bed. "I do not yet deserve your forgiveness, but I will act in such a way as to earn it. Here, let me start by carrying your things to the wagon. Then I will take you to the omnibus."

Masaru lifts the suitcase from the bed. "Heavy," he says.

"It's mostly full of books I'm returning to friends."

He looks so sad and uncertain that Kaede grants him an unintended smile and—she will wonder later how it could have happened without her willing it—opens her arms in welcome.

Masaru drops the suitcase on the floor, and they embrace, first tentatively and then passionately. Their passionate entanglement continues, and Masaru has just led Kaede to her bed, when her clock, chiming the time, cuts short the grip of lust.

"Oh, it's late! I've got to go, right now," she says as, standing now, she tucks her blouse back into her skirt and says, "Masaru, please put my suitcase in the wagon while I run to say good-bye to senhor Salles. He expects to drive me to the bus stop."

Masaru points at the Buddha's case. "I put Buddha in the wagon?"

"No, no, thank you," Kaede says. "I'll carry him to the wagon. I promised my father I would always keep the Buddha Amida with me."

Senhor Salles is disappointed; he had been looking forward to a long ride with Kaede, intending, as a surprise, to bypass the omnibus and drive her all the way to the universidade. But, feeling she should make her amorous decisions without outside pressure, he just smiles, gives her a long, heartfelt hug, and wishes her a safe journey.

Within the hour, Masaru and Kaede arrive at the bus stop, just in time.

"Here it comes," says Masaru. "Will you come back soon?"

"I still don't know," she replies. "But it will be just as soon as I can. It was in question for a while, but it is no longer. It's now a command of my heart. A command I dare not disobey."

Masaru helps Kaede down from the wagon, and as they approach the door of the bus, a hand reaches out and takes the suitcase from him. He turns back to Kaede, eager for a last embrace, and she leads him to the other side of the wagon, away from the eyes of passengers and driver. After placing Masaru's hands on her buttocks, she wraps her arms around him, draws him close, and kisses him with animal desire. She slides a thigh between his legs and they begin to rock, faster and faster until, Masaru reaches the finale he so urgently craved.

Kaede slips loose, takes a moment to gather her wits and tidy her hair and, after whispering, "Good, that will help us both with our dreams," she dashes onto the bus.

Riding back to the cafezal, Masaru drops the reins onto his lap, and the horse, focused on the hay that awaits it at home, increases its pace as Masaru repeats a mantra in rhythm with the gait of the horse: "She will be mine! She will be mine! She will be mine."

*

Arriving at São Paulo Centro hours late due to a road closure, Kaede looks for Roberto from her window as the bus is parking. Facing to the west, she notices the sun for the second time that day—half-risen when she woke in the morning, it is half-set now, leaving her feeling as if she has traveled half a world around.

Oh, here he comes, and he's smiling. Good. He must not be too upset at my being late. And as always, he looks so terribly handsome . . . but what makes him look that way? It's not how he dresses—that's neat, but certainly not decorative. It must be his facial features. They are so ornate—he reminds me of certain medieval statues, with his tall, broad forehead, square chin, and large, expressive lips. Roberto dear, I should ask him, have you ever modeled for Bernini? But oh, here he is.

Kaede steps from the bus and, after the usual exchange of Brasilian cheek kisses, left-left, right-right, they gather her luggage and board a taxi together.

"A Praça da Republica, por favor," Roberto says.

"I don't think we'll be able to enter the praça," says the driver. "There's a rally of some kind going on in there."

"Não problema," says Roberto. "Just leave us at the southern edge of the praça, and we'll go on by foot."

Later, still smiling over the delights of being repeatedly pitched into Kaede's arms as the driver jerked his taxi through the usual tangles of central São Paulo traffic, Roberto says, "You're just in time, Kaede. Today's crowd should be the biggest yet. The plumbers union just joined up with us, so we'll be celebrating that!"

On foot now, Kaede and Roberto weave their way through a sea of banners and signs to the stage at the center of the praça. On the stage, in addition to the usual PDP banners promoting liberty, equality, and fraternity, are some new banners that read:

PDP – Bem-vindo Encanadores – PDP. Welcome Plumbers.

And a new poster, one carried on sticks by a group encircling the stage—a poster ordered weeks ago by Kaede as a surprise for Roberto—features her favorite photo of him, standing with arms spread in his favorite victorious V, casting confidence with his smile, over the caption: PDP – Roberto Millefiore Para Senador – PDP.

A horn and drum band announces Roberto and Kaede's appearance on stage, where Candido and a few others await them. One takes Kaede's suitcase, locking it in the musical instrument cage for safekeeping, while the Buddha Amida, as usual, remains supported by her hip and shoulder.

The mostly young crowd cheers wildly when someone hands Roberto a microphone. He steps forward with arms raised high, welcomes all present, then reads a special welcome prepared by Kaede. The welcome, along with conventional greetings and assertions of brotherhood between the PDP and the plumbers, praises the plumbers as the hope of the people. For they have the will and they have the tools to rid Brasil of the many clots, introduced by the government, that have for so long blocked the flow of benefits to the workers who have rightly earned them.

As the cheers die down, Roberto says, "And next, I want to congratulate you all on the good luck that has come your way today. Many of you, I know, arrived resigned to having to endure another of my endless speeches. But today, by the grace of your guardian angels, I will hardly speak at all." Over a ripple of laughter, Roberto goes on. "Today I will simply ask you to come with me, all of you, to the *Palaço Presidençial*, where the junta is about to make an important announcement. Let our presence and our voices serve as encouragement to those brave leaders in their efforts to promote democracy in our beloved Brasil!

"But first, before we march, let me introduce the newcomers to dona Kaede Miroka, Secretária da Partida Democratica Popular, who has come from the interior of the state, all the way from Aruja, to march with us today."

Roberto extends a hand toward Kaede, who bows in thanks as the crowd chants,

"Bem-vinda, dona Kaede! Bem-vinda, dona Kaede! Bem-vinda, dona Kaede!"

Then, at a signal from Roberto, the bandmaster starts the band, and the march begins, with Roberto, Kaede, and Candida leading the crowd down the avenida.

*

On an early August morning, sunny but cool for the time of year, about a dozen workers, senhor Salles, the family doctor, and a Shinto priest stand about a freshly filled grave at Cafezal Tres Lagos's cemetery.

Kyoami, kneeling at the foot of the grave, sobs into his hands as the priest, resplendent in a crystal-blue skirt overlaid by an open golden robe, stands at the head of the grave, next to a statue of the Buddha Gautama sitting under the Bo tree.

The Buddha Gautama had been Kyoami's grandmother's favorite of all the Hindu gods. The statue had been badly stained and chipped by the casinha fire, but Kyoami and his girlfriend beautifully restored it, or reincarnated it, as the girlfriend chose to put it, and the grandmother chose to believe.

The priest, standing tall in high heels and a woolen beehive hat, reads a number of prayers from an ancient manuscript then rolls the parchment back onto its bamboo spool and ties it with a scarlet ribbon in a ritual pattern. After bowing to each person present, the priest recites one more prayer from memory. When he leaves the cemetery, two little boys run alongside him, carrying the hem of his skirt above the wooden path that Masaru constructed for the occasion.

As the priest leaves, Kyoami stands, wipes the tears from his face, and is embraced by senhor Salles, who whispers condolences and departs.

Masaru is next. After bowing to Kyoami, he says, "Your grandmother remains a precious spirit, happy now in the Pure Land in the company of the Buddha she loves so much."

Then Masaru moves aside and the other workers step forward, one by one, and offer their condolences as well.

Later, walking back to the casa da cafezal, senhor Salles turns to the doctor and says, "Antonio, I have been wondering. Were you ever able to determine the exact cause of the senhora's death?"

"No, not with certainty, Pedroso. All I know for sure is that her heart stopped beating. But I don't know why. It may have simply stopped of old age and caused her fall from her chair. On the other hand, she was so old and fragile, she may simply have fallen off her stool for lack of balance. The impact of hitting the ground might have stopped her heart in itself. One explanation seems as likely as the other."

"I see. Thank you, Antonio, and thank you for coming all this way to help us. I know how busy you are."

"No thanks required, Pedroso. For friends like you, I am always available, and always pleased to be of assistance."

"Well, in any case, I hope you can stay for tea. The cook has made some of her French croissants which, if I remember correctly, are favorites of yours."

"Ah, Pedroso, your memory is good, and my propensity to gluttony remains intact. Unfortunately, I must rush back to my hospital to tend to an urgent case. But I will soon return to accept your offer."

"All right then, until next time, Antonio. And for next time, let's also plan on fishing for *dourado*s. I know a stream where a huge one awaits you."

"A huge *dourado* and French croissants, and both on one visit! The temptations you offer are too great to resist, my friend. You may see me sooner than you think."

As Antonio drives away, Masaru approaches senhor Salles and says, "Ah, senhor, Kyoami's grandmother was of great age."

"Yes, she was, Masaru. Kyoami says he thinks she was ninety-three."

"Such a long life! Did she ever tell who burned their casinha?"

"No, unfortunately, she didn't. But I continue to hope to learn the culprit's identity. Are you still asking?"

"I still ask, senhor. I ask and wait. I ask and wait. Someone will tell me, I am sure."

9

A Kiss in the Dark

It is already late afternoon when Kaede and Roberto, ravenous and in search of lunch, settle at a sidewalk café in the northern city of Manaus. The café borders a small plaza, at the center of which a bronze horse carries a sword-waving rider dressed in an ancient uniform. And to the horse there is tethered a monkey—a hungry monkey it turns out, it being late for lunch and early for dinner. So the monkey, as soon as it sees Kaede and Roberto seat themselves, begins his much-practiced performance, which includes leaping acrobatics, followed by mimicking the catching and eating of food, complete with postprandial licking of fingertips and lips.

"Oh, it's good to sit," says Kaede. "It's been such a long day."

"Yes, a long day indeed," says Roberto. "But a good day too. The crowds were wonderful!"

"And we didn't even get rained on like they predicted. But tell me, Roberto, did the police really mean it when they said they wouldn't allow us to enter the Opera House, even if it did rain? Sometimes it comes down really hard around here."

"Yes, I think they did mean it. Here in the interior, it's usual for the police to enforce whatever orders they get from the local powers. And, of course, we represent an unwelcome challenge to those powers, so … But here comes our waiter."

Kaede orders fried chicken with garlic and olive oil, and a glass of sauvignon blanc.

"Sim, senhora. And senhor?"

"I see that you're featuring grilled *jaraqui*, my favorite fish. Is it fresh?"

"Absolutely. Fresh and beautiful, I might add. My ten-year-old son caught it this morning, with an arrow launched from his canoe. His first arrow catch of anything big, except for bottom dwellers."

"Well then, that's for me. And a glass of sauvignon blanc for me too, please."

Wine and bread and butter are served at once, and the monkey is promptly tossed his allotment. Kaede and Roberto sip wine and watch the nightly parade of dressed-up teenage girls slowly circumambulate the square, mock-shyly displaying their charms for the boys who casually sit around, pretending not to notice the girls, while whispering excited comparisons to each other.

"So, Roberto, how does it feel to hear them yelling, 'Viva Roberto Senador! Viva Roberto Senador!' over and over, like they did today?"

"Exciting, of course, but ultimately it feels more like dreaming than existing. Still, who knows? The dream just might come true."

" 'Just might?' Only 'just might'? I've been thinking, *surely will*. In fact, I've been feeling as I imagine Josephine felt while watching her Bonaparte make history. Though, of course, you're taller than Bonaparte, and handsomer by far. And, ha! Since we've been sitting here, I've even been having visions of you replacing the Portuguese swordsman on that brass horse over there."

"Ha, indeed," says Roberto. "There are better uses for brass than that. And I'm not so sure I'd like to serve as tethering for that particular monkey. But it is exciting to be part of such a historic time."

"And you, as the first senador from the PDP, will be one of the main architects of that history!"

"*If* they allow it."

" '*If* they allow it.' There you go again. Who is 'they,' and why all the pessimistic insecurity? That's not at all like you. It seems certain to me that you *will* get the votes."

"Oh yes, I and some of our other candidates will get the votes, no question about that. But will the votes be properly counted? *That* is the question."

"Roberto, you've been working too hard on this campaign. It's making you unreasonable, if not outright paranoid. Why wouldn't the votes be properly counted? You heard the Marechal himself promise free elections, with the voting closely supervised by the army."

"Yes, I heard him. And the Marechal, I'm convinced, is incorruptible. The army will closely supervise, and mainly, those who are eligible will be allowed to vote, and votes will be limited to one vote per voter. But unfortunately, it's not the army but the bureaucracy—that demon child so long corrupted—that is charged with *counting* the votes."

"But can't the Marechal control the bureaucracy?"

"Probably not. It has been around too long and has grown too extensive. It's become like a great fungal net that grows underground continuously, popping up to the surface only to gather rainfall—in this case, falling bribes—after which it slips back underground to await the next downpour."

"Have you actually heard from them, from the bureaucrats? Have they said how much they want?"

"Only indirectly, and only approximately, in shifting figures. But the message is clear. They will guarantee a fair count, *if we pay enough*. And *enough*, of course, simply means more than the opposition."

"But surely we wouldn't pay them even if we had the money, would we, Roberto? I mean, paying bala to introduce democracy seems, well, awfully close to prostitution."

"It is awfully close to prostitution, Kaede. But what else can we do? Paying to have the votes properly counted is deplorable, I'll grant you. But the alternative, letting the powers that be defeat the will of the people with the very money they've stolen from the people, would be even more deplorable. Not only would the people lose this election, but they'd probably also lose—for who knows how long—the motivation to try again."

"Awful, awful, awful. So what should we do, Roberto?"

"Well, for now, no matter how unlikely, raising enough money to ensure a proper count has to be our first priority. Then, after winning the election, we can go to work uprooting the bureaucracy."

"But how will we know how much we will need?"

"We have a few spies within the bureaucracy but, since the power elite are the richest in the land, we're really scared that we wont be able to match-plus their offer.

"But what if we did 'match-plus their offer'? Wouldn't they just up the ante once again?"

"I'm sure they would if they got the chance, but we might be able to outmaneuver them if we have the cash to begin with. We have a little plan that just might work out."

"What's that?"

"We would wait until the very last moment, when the votes are in but not yet counted. Then—after the Marechal arranges some phone outages and road closures and a bit of shortwave interference—we would outbid the powers' last offer, while the Marechal's soldiers stick around for the count, until the deadline passes.

"It should work, since the bureaucrats will believe they have the best money already in hand. And an apparently proper count at that point, with the Marechal's soldiers right there, will also relieve the bureaucrats of the worry that the Marechal might make trouble later on by calling for a recount. Anyway, that's the plan I suggested to the Marechal, and he said he likes it."

"Okay. But I thought you said you weren't sure we could even outbid the opposition in the first place."

"It's worse than that. I'm *almost sure,* at an intuitive level, that we won't be able to outbid them. At least, not unless we find some really significant new money. That's why I sound so pessimistic, despite our plan. But still, there are a few possibilities we haven't looked into that just might make the difference. One of which I'm hoping you can help with."

"Me? How so?"

"I was wondering if you, as a 'Nipponese,' could approach the Nippo-Brasilians of Aruja, and maybe the residents of some of the other Nipponese enclaves, for community donations. "I've already solicited the Italo-Brasilian organizations, and they gave very generously. But since they mostly represent poor workers who ran away from Mussolini, and who don't save very well anyway, the actual amounts weren't very large. So now I'm hoping that the Nippo-Brasilians, with their well-known passion for saving, and with all the success they've had introducing and marketing new crops, might be able to give us more."

Kaede frowns in dismay. "Oh, how I *wish* I could help with that! But I'm afraid I won't be able to. Not in Aruja or in any of the other enclaves."

"How so? It seems to me the Nippo-Brasilians have everything to gain from the institution of democracy, given how marginalized and isolated they are."

"It may seem that way, Roberto, but the truth is that the Nipponese of the enclaves remain isolated by their own choice. And though it's also true that they work hard and save passionately, they're not doing it to ensure a better life in Brasil. They're doing it to *get out of Brasil* as soon as they feel financially secure enough. You, Roberto, like most people, refer to them as 'Nippo-Brasilians,' but that isn't how they think of themselves. They think of themselves as Nipponese only. Nipponese temporarily displaced from their homeland by economic ill fortune. The only government they want to support is that of His Divinity the Crane, as they call Emperor Hirohito."

"I could understand all of that, Kaede, except for a couple of crucial elements. Such as: how can they mean to return to Imperial Nippon, when the whole world knows that Imperial Nippon no longer exists? And how can they ignore the fact that Hirohito has surrendered his empire, renounced his divinity, and has agreed to accept a constitution for his country that will introduce democratic reforms and, it is said, perpetual demilitarization? Everyone knows these things, so it's hard for me to believe that the residents of even the more remote enclaves aren't aware of them."

"You're right, Roberto, they are aware of what is being said. But the older Nipponese, and even most of their children—who are in the habit of listening carefully to what their parents tell them—nonetheless believe that Nippon has won the war. That's what being isolated in enclaves is all about. It's what's called holding onto your culture and believing what you want to believe."

"But—but the Allied victory and the defeat of Nippon are such completely public knowledge. How can anyone choose not to believe it?"

"It *is* all public knowledge, Roberto, but public knowledge as accepted in most of Brasil is not public knowledge as accepted in the enclaves. There they read only their own press, attend only their own schools, and listen only to their elders, many of whom are members of the secret Loyalists society.

"Historical truth is one thing, but culturally acceptable truth is something else. Ultimately, the enclavists are like most people. What they believe is what they want to believe. Nothing more, nothing less. The difference between them and most other people is just that—at least in matters having to do with culture and nationality—they are more committed to what they want to believe than most. Besides which, in this particular case, they have good arguments to use to counter stories of Nippon's defeat."

"Such as?"

"Well, for instance, if you ask the elders or any Loyalist why they don't believe there's been an Allied victory, they'll remind you that, *within their own lifetimes,* the Imperial forces of Nippon have: defeated the Chinese twice, defeated the Russians, annexed Korea, and occupied not only Manchuria, but most of East Asia and the Western Pacific as well. And, for good measure, they'll remind you that the Nipponese not so long ago sank much of the American Navy at Pearl Harbor.

"It's a bit too absurd, they will tell you, for the Allies now to claim that Nippon has been defeated by the very countries it so recently conquered. Such a story, they will insist, can only be the type of propaganda disseminated by the desperate. That is to say, a fabrication so extravagant that reasonable people will tend to say it must be true, because no one would dare tell that big a lie! In short, the Loyalists consider the story of Nippon's defeat as nothing but a cover-up for an Allied defeat.

"And as for the emperor renouncing his divinity, they will ask you, again with perfect logic, by what means could the emperor, as a direct descendant of the sun goddess Amaterasu Omikami, possibly renounce his divinity? Divinity is, by definition, an eternal. It is an essence, not an office that one can take up or leave at will."

"Well, Kaede, I have to admit, as wrong as their arguments may be, they are cogent ones."

"Exactly. That's what allows them to say with certainty, that in this case, their reasoning prevails over Brasilian propaganda."

"But surely there are *some* in the Nippo-Brasilian community who recognize Nippon's defeat as historical fact."

"Sure, there are some. They are called the Defeatists by the Loyalists, who think of themselves, as the name indicates, as loyal subjects of the emperor. Among other things, they are dedicated to eliminating the Defeatists."

"The Loyalists are dedicated to 'eliminating' the Defeatists? What do you mean by 'eliminating'? "

"I mean they are intent on silencing them by getting them out of the culture, one way or the other. And it appears that no means are necessarily beyond them."

"And the Loyalists outnumber the Defeatists?"

"By far, though nobody knows what the real numbers are, because both the Loyalists and the Defeatists keep their identities secret. The Defeatists do so to avoid the wrath of the Loyalists, and the Loyalists do so to better spy on and persecute the Defeatists."

"So the Loyalists actually persecute their own people."

"Sometimes in horrifying ways. For instance, it seems pretty clear that one of senhor Salles's workers had his house burned down by the Loyalists simply for letting it leak that he thought the Allies had won the war."

"Horrifying indeed! I had no idea. And of course, if you add enough fear to suspicion, then suspicion becomes conviction, which, in this case, leads to persecution.

"But tell me: You're not in any *personal* danger, are you?"

"Personal danger? I'm happy to report that, so far, I'm pretty calm about that, since there hasn't been any direct aggression aimed at me, even though as a graduate of a Brasilian university, I'm automatically suspect. Mostly, I think, I've been left in peace because I'm protected by who my father was, and also because of my relationship with senhor Salles, who supports the independence of the enclaves, and who likes to refer to me in public as his daughter."

Their meals arrive, and Kaede and Roberto eat in pensive silence. With the coming of nightfall, an attendant lights a score of lanterns, and a large white statue of St. Sebastian comes to life on a nearby platform. The lanterns, always carefully positioned, illuminate the many arrows that pierce the martyr and display his bleeding wounds that continuously ooze sainted blood, painted afresh by the faithful each Saturday night.

Later in the week, Kaede, her day's work done, is sitting at a table outside a cabaret in Porto Alegré, just steps away from the surf. Halfway through her second glass of wine, her spirit is afloat, drifting with the moonlit clouds as the plaintive vocals of the *fado* tell a tragic story of lost love. Finally the fadoist, the beautiful granddaughter of two slaves, finishes a flawless performance and bows in thanks for the enthusiastic applause that follows.

Roberto, who had been waiting for the performance to end, now walks through the cabaret to Kaede's table.

He looks sad, sad as the fado sounded, Kaede thinks as she rises to embrace him.

They sit, a waiter promptly appears, and Roberto orders a double *pinga* — palm brandy.

Kaede declines more wine and, as soon as the waiter leaves, says, "Roberto. You're having a *double pinga*? I've never seen you drink anything that strong before."

"And you've never seen me quite this upset before, either."

"Oh, Roberto, darling, what is it?"

"I've just come from talking to our accountant, and it turns out that financially, things could hardly be worse. Our spy got the figure for the initial offer that the opposition has made to the bureaucrats, and it's more than twice the best we were even *hoping* to raise! And that would be if we get a second emergency donation that we're negotiating with the transit workers."

"And there are no other possibilities?"

"None that I can see. At least, none of significance."

"That's terrible, Roberto, terrible! I've been trying to think up new ideas myself, but the only one that's come to me has been to ask senhor Salles. I know he's sympathetic to our cause but, as a major coffee plantation owner, if he did contribute, he'd be branded a traitor by his own cohort. So it doesn't seem fair to ask him."

"I agree, Kaede, it wouldn't be fair. But here we are, badly stuck, only a few weeks before the elections, with hope fading fast. *That's* why I'm so upset."

When the waiter brings Roberto his drink, Kaede orders a double pinga for herself. She meets her first sip with a grimace, but then, sipping more slowly, she joins Roberto, watching the ocean play with the moon's reflection. They order two more doubles, which they toss right down, after which Roberto places money on the table and asks the waiter to call a taxi.

Their ride soon arrives, and Roberto and Kaede, sliding to and fro as the taxi negotiates a series of rough and tumbled roads, sit tipsy-close, arms around each other's shoulders, until the taxi stops in front of a house with a sign in its yard that reads, Bem-vinda a Pensão Gato Feliz (Welcome to the Happy Cat Boardinghouse).

"Do they really have a happy cat?" Roberto asks.

"They do have a cat, but considering the way he skulks about, I think he'd be better named Surly Cat."

Roberto chuckles, asks the driver to wait, and says, "I'll walk you to your door, Kaede."

As Roberto steps from the taxi ahead of Kaede, he is momentarily blinded by the headlights of a car parking close behind. He stumbles on the curb and falls. Promptly righting himself, he pulls up a trouser leg and looks at the injured skin.

"Are you okay?" Kaede asks, as the headlights go out and darkness returns.

"Yes, I'm okay," says Roberto, rubbing his knee. "It's just a minor bruise."

They walk to the porch of the pension, where they talk for a few minutes about their schedules, hug several times, exchange a lengthy kiss, and separate.

Roberto is turning to leave when Kaede gives him a fetching smile and a slow wink, to which he responds by drawing her close once more. They go mouth to mouth and tongue to tongue this time, with a passion that intertwines them both.

They linger, kissing and hugging and radiating affection, until Roberto—who is thrilled, but also overwhelmed by the combination of political stress, unaccustomed brandy, and surprisingly sexuality—says, "I'll call you tomorrow as soon as I know when the emergency financial meeting will be. There'll be a few new people there that the transits are bringing. Maybe one of them will have a brilliant last-minute idea."

Kaede nods in agreement. She turns away but then turns back, gives Roberto a lustful grin, waves good night, and disappears into the house.

Roberto walks back to the taxi and climbs in, saying, *"Dos centos rua São Clemente, por favor."* (Two hundred Saint Clemente street, please.)

The taxi driver says, "Sim, senhor," and pulls away from the curb. They have a long way to go, across most of the city, but it's late, traffic is light, and the driver, as is common practice in the city, slows but does not stop for red lights. Before long, he stops the taxi on Saint Clement Street. "Are we here?" he asks, searching for a house number.

Roberto is uncertain, for the lights that illuminate the front of his building are out, although that is not an unusual event. But then a passing car rescues his building from the dark, and Roberto steps from the taxi. He passes money through the driver's window, waits for the right change, adds a tip, and heads for his building.

Approaching the front door with keys in hand, Roberto is startled by the sudden appearance of a large man, who steps from beneath a low awning and strides quickly toward him. Pivoting on his heel, Roberto discovers a second man, this one with a length of pipe in hand, approaching from behind.

"What is it?" Roberto demands. "What do you want!"

"For now," the man in front replies, "we want only to give you a little advice. Quit the race for senador. That's all, *just quit the race*. And to help you remember our advice, here are a few more kisses to add to your total for the night."

The man in front nods to the man behind, and Roberto has only time to shout once for help before a blow to the skull drops him to the ground.

The night is dark, but it is warm, and through open windows, Roberto's neighbors hear him call for the neighborhood guard, followed by the sounds of muted blows, moans and groans, running footsteps, slamming car doors, and a screeching departure.

Several neighbors wait a few minutes and then, hearing nothing further, rush outside. A flashlight pans over Roberto's broken body as someone says, "Look at all the blood! He's in bad shape, that one!"

Another says, "Where is that damned guard? "I saw him earlier, patrolling on his bicycle with his pistol in the basket."

"He's useless," says another. "I don't know why we pay him. But c'mon, we've got to do something for this poor guy. There's an emergency center about a kilometer away."

"I know the one," the man with the flashlight says "I'll drive over. No point in trying to call, my phone's been out for days. You keep watch, and I'll go get them."

Kaede, meanwhile, is engulfed by erotic dreams with Roberto's visage as foreground, background, and center. They come and go until late in the morning, when someone from the PDP bangs upon her bedroom door.

A nurse leads Kaede to Roberto's room, which he shares with a double amputee. The amputee, a young man, was hitching a ride from an omnibus by hanging onto an open window while riding his bicycle—a frightening but common sight in São Paulo, one that often results in similar consequences. In this case, the young man was sent askew by a pothole and then run over by another omnibus, which had been closely trailing the first.

"When your friend is awake, it will be all right to talk with him," the nurse tells Kaede, "though he's heavily opiated and may not make much sense. But please speak softly. His roommate needs whatever sleep he can get."

Kaede nods, thanks the nurse, and peeks behind the curtain that shields Roberto's bed from the next. His scalp and chin are heavily bandaged; his right hand and forearm, as well as the lower part of his right leg, are enclosed in plaster casts; and an IV drip feeds a vein in his left arm. Kaede puts a chair near the head of his bed and sits, waiting for him to wake.

It's a short wait, but when Roberto's eyes do open, they are vacant. He gestures to be elevated, and Kaede slowly cranks his bed into a half-sitting position, his lack of response leaving her to guess that will do.

Leaning close, she says, "Oh, Roberto, you've been hurt so badly!"

He apparently hears her, since he looks straight at her, though the vacancy in his eyes remains. But then, after some minutes, he squints, tilts his head, and gradually, recognition enters his eyes.

"Roberto, it's me, Kaede. Don't you recognize me?"

"Sure I recognize you. You're Kaede, just like you said. It's just that I'm not used to your wings. You must not wear them very often, because I've never seen them before. And that compass on top of your head. I've never seen it before, either. It's a nice one, too, though that doesn't really matter for compasses. All that really matters is whether it's pointing the way it's supposed to. Is it pointing north? I can't tell from here. And why are you wearing it? Did you use it to find me?"

"Oh, Roberto, are you in much pain?"

"No, not really. I think they must have cut the pain away. And the damage isn't as bad as it looks. The doctor said that ... What was it? Oh, that's right. He said that I'll be able to go home pretty soon, though he said I'll need assistance."

"I am that assistance."

"Thank you, Kaede. But where ... where? Oh, there you are. What happened to your compass? Did it spin away?"

"Who did this to you, Roberto?"

"I don't know. I can't remember. I remember paying a taxi driver. Then I woke up here. Is this São Paulo General?"

"Yes."

"Good. That's the test, you know. If you can tell them where you are, then you're okay. I heard them say that to someone in the hall."

"That's great, and I'm sure they're right. You're going to be just fine. But going back to your attack. You can't remember it. Okay, but how about the police? Have you talked to them?"

"They were here. But they said they ..." His eyes close.

Alarmed, Kaede presses a buzzer attached to Roberto's bed, and a nurse promptly pops through the doorway. "Sim, senhora?"

"He fell asleep right while he was talking. Is he all right?"

The nurse takes Roberto's pulse, lifts his lids, and listens to his breathing. "It's nothing," she says. "Just the narcotic. A common side effect."

"He was seeing things too. He thought I had angel wings, and a compass on my head."

"The narcotic again. Hallucinations. Free movies, we call them here. But I'll turn it down a bit," she says, reaching for the IV valve. "At least he saw you as an angel and not a fanged demon, like they sometimes do," she giggles.

"Also, nurse, can you tell me his prognosis?"

"No, I can't do that. But I'll ask the resident to talk to you about it."

"Thank you. Also, I 'd like to stay overnight. Could you arrange a cot for me?"

"Oh, of that I'm not sure. It would be highly irregular. I would have to ask my supervisor."

Kaede rummages about in her purse, finds some money, and slips it to the nurse. "Yes, please ask your supervisor. That would be kind of you."

While waiting for the nurse to return, Kaede lifts a folded copy of *O Journal do Rio* from Roberto's nightstand and opens it. The front page is totally filled by a large photo of Roberto and a related article. *Thank God the picture's from before the assault. Good picture too! They must have copied it from one of the posters I had made for him.*

The accompanying article is well written, but finally disappointing in that it concludes with statements from the police chiefs of both city and state, who say they have no suspects in the case but ask the public to send in any possibly relevant information. Anonymity preserved.

Ha! A person would have to be awfully naïve—or suicidal—to trust that anonymity would hold in a case of this political importance. Or to assume any safety in appearing as a witness.

She still remembers her father warning her, when she was about to get her driver's license, about the country's legal system. If she were to have a serious accident, or even witness one, he explained, she would immediately become *en flagrante*—a legal term meaning that, if caught within twenty-four hours, she might be considered responsible for the accident and would be held a prisoner until a court decided her fate. A highly problematic situation, he pointed out, since her hearing might be months away. In other words, he told her: "You are presumed to be guilty until proven innocent."

Her father's advice, which he stated most forcefully, had been that in the case of serious accident, she was to leave the scene immediately and come directly to him or a trusted friend who would hide her for at least twenty-four hours. After which, being no longer considered *en flagrante*, she could go to the authorities with a lawyer to tell them whatever she knew.

She recalls, with residual shame, the day when, not long after her father's warning, she came upon a body bleeding in the street. She did not dare stop to see if she could help, but drove home as instructed. Her father and senhor Salles took her to a mountain resort for the week-end, after which she testified.

Returning to *O Journal,* Kaede realizes that, given the sympathetic tone of the article on Roberto, as well as his handsome and honest appearance, the article should, on the whole, have a positive effect on voters.

She folds the paper back up and lays it aside just as a porter enters the room with a cot. She has him set the cot flush alongside Roberto's bed then lies on it to test it. It's pretty hard, and lower than Roberto's bed, but she manages to roll from it onto the bed and back, so good enough.

Kaede's mind wants desperately to vanish in sleep, the previous night's good rest notwithstanding. She wants to escape her fears about Roberto, and she wants that escape right now. But first, she experiments with a single butterfly kiss on his cheek. Seeing no reaction, she covers all of the visible parts of his face with a flock of kisses. She then stretches his blanket over both of them, turns off all but the nightlight, and joins her lover in sleep.

Ten days later, Roberto is in bed in his apartment, propped up on pillows, with Kaede massaging his feet from a perch on the edge of his bed. Continuing their conversation, Roberto says, "They may think the angel wings and compass were just hallucinations, but I say they were part of a spiritual vision. A peek at the essence behind what passes for real. Not that the way you usually look isn't gorgeous to begin with. And if you doubt the story, let me point out that there's a tip-off, right here and now, that the view was true."

"And the tip-off is?"

"The wings and compass are gone, but the angel remains."

"Oh, how sad! To have lost my wings and my compass both, all at once, and so soon after I got them. How will I ever get around?"

"Yes, it is sad, but it's also reassuring to me. Wingless angels can't fly away."

"As if one would fly away from such a flatterer."

Hugs and kisses follow in a stream, mixed with loving tears.

"But now, dear Roberto, it's time for you to rest. Will you need your sleeping pills?"

"I think not. Last night I forgot to take them and slipped right off without them. But leave a couple here on the table, just in case. Not more than two, though. I'm always afraid that, being too groggy to remember I've already had two, I might take two more, and two more, and so on. I've heard that sometimes happens."

"Here they are. Sweet dreams, my love, sweet dreams. I'll be here when you wake." Kaede moves Roberto's extra pillows out of the way, fluffs the remaining one, and slides it under his head. She closes his eyes with her fingertips, kisses each of his lids, turns off his lamp, and leaves the room.

Later, in her nightshirt, she studies Roberto's sleeping figure. *Lovely, lovely, even all beat-up.* She slithers into bed and snuggles her body toward his, just close enough to feel the warmth of him, without quite touching, and enters dreamland through the portal Roberto left open for her.

*

Hundreds of northeasterners have gathered on the beach at the Bay of All Saints to celebrate the annual feast of Iemanjá, the Orixa goddess of the sea and fertility. Mostly descendants of African slaves, they will eat and drink and dance and sing the whole night through, in happy communion with the goddess. The drinks and treats are unusually splendid in both quantity and quality this year, largely by grace of donations from the PDP.

The music, though, apart from loaned equipment, is entirely the celebrants' provision. And provide they do, in sessions so long and strenuous as to defy the limits of human energy, proof, it is believed, that the music comes from the goddess Herself.

The PDP, having decided to avoid any speeches at what is, after all, a sacred party, has limited its expression to planting four banners, one at each corner of the great rectangle that the authorities have specified as the party's legal geographic limits.

One of the banners, waving in a gentle sea breeze, reads, PDP Bahianas e Bahianos Beba Com Iemanjá! PDP (Bahianas and Bahianos Drink with Iemanjá!) Other banners exhort the celebrants to dance and sing and love with Iemanjá.

As a copper sun collaborates with a deep blue sea to form a violet sky, six young women sing a message of love to the watery horizon, while six young men with silver ropes dangling from their waists step into the water. The young men fasten their ropes to a bamboo raft the women have piled high with drinks and fruits and flowers and candies and perfume.

As the women end their song with wind-cast kisses, the young men, swimming three to a side, tow the raft out to sea. They swim until they meld with the horizon, and there they stop and untie their ropes. Being careful to disturb the water as little as possible, they then swim some meters away and watch as the goddess, rising from the depths, grasps the raft from below and guides it down, down, down to her deep-water mountain home, where her court waits to share the people's gifts with her.

The swimmers return to shore, where all toast the goddess with a special brandy made from a recipe known only to a few Macumba priests—priests of a religious cult—which is drunk only on this day each year, and only to fete the goddess. It is the same brandy that she, from the tallest of the peaks surrounding her underwater mountain home, raises to return the celebrants' toast.

*

It is late at night, under a dark and moonless sky, when a small truck pulls up to the curb in front of Roberto's apartment building. The driver jumps out and thoroughly checks the grounds by flashlight. Finding no one, he opens the vehicle's rear gate and slides out a ramp, connecting the truck bed to the ground.

Roberto descends the ramp in his wheelchair, and Kaede starts to push it along for him, but he says, "No thanks. I need to practice doing this alone."

With one hand still in a cast, he awkwardly propels himself down the walk, while the driver runs ahead to unlock the building's front door. After carefully inspecting both the outside of the building and the hallway leading to Roberto's apartment, the driver holds the front door open for Roberto and Kaede to pass.

"What time should I fetch you in the morning?" asks the driver.

"At seven, please."

The three exchange good nights, and the driver departs. Roberto, his hurt arm cramping from the effort of wheeling himself, now asks Kaede to push him down the hall. And as she pushes, the darkness within the apartment is pierced by a flashlight beam. The beam scans a wall and stops at the door of an armoire. A slim hand opens the armoire, revealing a number of dresses and robes hanging side by side along a single pole.

The hand slowly separates hangers, then stops midway and isolates a single hanger from its neighbors.

The light pauses on the hanger, which supports an exquisite silver kimono, its neck a ring of golden dogwood blossoms intertwined on an indigo collar, which lead to the vines that connect the many jewels that twinkle along the rest of the robe.

The intruder hisses and whispers harshly: "She even wears her mother's kimono for him!"

Then, through the locked door, he hears Kaede say, "I'm exhausted."

"Me too," he hears Roberto say. "I'm desperate to lie down."

The intruder turns off the flashlight as Kaede puts a key in the lock, saying: "I'll turn on a light, and be right back."

She opens the door and steps one foot into the apartment, a little off balance as she reaches for the wall switch, when a body slams her back through the doorway and into the hall.

Crashing into Roberto's wheelchair, she knocks it onto its side as a hooded figure charges from the apartment and disappears down the hall and out of the building. She staggers to her feet, rights Roberto's wheelchair, helps him back into it and, staring into his eyes, asks, "Are you all right?"

"Yes, I think so. But not you, you're bleeding." He touches her scalp and holds up his fingertips for her to see. "Look at this blood!"

"It's nothing," she replies, fingering the cut. "It feels like a little skin wound."

After locking the wheels on Roberto's wheelchair, Kaede enters the apartment alone. She turns on all the lights and inspects each room and closet. In the armoire in the bedroom, she notices that her clothes have been disturbed, with her mother's kimono in isolation from the rest of her clothes.

Seeing nothing else irregular, she returns to the hall and wheels Roberto into the apartment. After locking and bolting the front door, she helps him out of his chair and onto the couch. "Are you truly all right?" she asks.

"Yes, truly," he says. "A bit shaken, of course, but otherwise all right. But I'm still worried about your cut."

She leaves the room and comes back minutes later with a clean forehead and a blood-tinged washrag in her hand. She kneels before Roberto and shows him a fine red line on her scalp. "You see . . . it's nothing. Just a child's play cut."

Roberto, leaning over, kisses her skin near the cut, and Kaede, still feeling the shock of the hit, sits on the floor and lays her head in his lap.

"I'm glad you're not seriously hurt," he says, "but even so, this state of affairs cannot continue. Seriously hurt this time or not, you might have been, and you may be, if and when there is a next time."

"I don't think anyone meant to hurt me, Roberto. I was just in the way. It's you they want to hurt. You've got to get some bodyguards."

"Whether they intend to hurt you is not the point, Kaede. As we've just seen, simply being in the way is dangerous enough. We will have to find a way to ensure your safety. And you're right, of course. I should have bodyguards, and I won't pretend I'm not afraid, but also, like it or not, I need to set an example. Bodyguards would make me feel safer, but they would also advertise my fear to a public unaccustomed to such precautions. And seeing my fear might add to their own—workers are victims of so many threats—and they might skip the vote.

"You have to admit, first-time voters, publicly voting against rulers whom they know from experience to be ruthless, have reason enough to be afraid."

"But Roberto, this makes *twice* you've been attacked. The next time you may die. And tell me, what good would a *dead* Roberto be?"

"Yes, of course, you're right. I might die next time. But I won't, and even if I did, you would be my replacement. That's already understood and agreed upon by the staff of the PDP. And you, being at least as dedicated and able as I, and being sheltered by senhor Salles to boot, would become the first elected senadora in Brasil. The people, in the end, would win."

"Please don't talk that way, Roberto. If you should die—Oh, Roberto, I don't know! I don't know if I could carry on at all, let alone run for senadora."

"Kaede, if I should die, you *would* carry on. I know that, because you are here now, doing everything you can for your chosen country, even though you understand the dangers. You've not run off to the USA or wherever to wait things out, despite the menace of the Loyalists. You *would* carry on, I know, because you are a brave person who cares about the people."

She shakes her head. "Roberto, we shouldn't talk so freely of your possible demise. It's exactly that kind of talk that attracts the demons of death."

"Demons of death? *Demons of death*? I should worry about being overheard by demons of death? In nineteen hundred and forty-nine? Ah, hah hah!"

"The demons of death are not a joke, Roberto, they exist! And they often bring death to those who slight them. It is their mission. I know! It was they, the demons of death, who drove my mother to end her life. She told me so herself!"

"I'm sorry, Kaede. I'm sorry. I didn't realize you were being so serious. But how can you believe that demons …?"

"Roberto, before you start laughing at everything you don't comprehend, just ask yourself how many times you have thought something unlikely to happen, or even thought something could not happen, when, presto, just like that, it *did?*"

"Mmm, admittedly, several times."

"And have you ever heard voices? Maybe unclear voices, as in entering or emerging from dreams, voices that maybe returned to follow you during the day?"

"A few times."

"Demons again. Just because you don't understand something doesn't mean it isn't there. Do you think your heart beats just to please you?"

"Okay, Kaede, okay. Again, I'm sorry I ridiculed your concerns. I'll be more careful in the future. But still, it's clear that you're at too great a risk whenever you're with me in private. So from now on, we'll have to avoid being together alone.

"Also, though I won't get bodyguards, I'll quit this apartment, I'll keep my schedule secret, and I'll sleep in a different place every night until the election is over."

Kaede leans forward, places her hands on Roberto's cheeks, and kisses him lushly on the mouth.

Smiling, she says, "Yes, all right. We'll separate whenever we're not in public. Beginning tomorrow, that is."

"Yes, that's right, beginning tomorrow."

10

The Buddha Returns

Roberto arrives at Aguaçu Falls early in the morning, having secured permission to arrive before the public opening hour. His driver opens his door and extends his arms to help.

"That's okay," Roberto says, "I can make it. I've been practicing. Watch this."

Turning sideways in his seat, he plants his cane on the ground between his knees, straightens his legs, slips forward from his seat, leans over his cane, and stands up straight. He rocks in place a bit, finds his balance, and grins in satisfaction.

"Very good!" exclaims the driver, clapping.

They walk to the top of a descending column of stairs, where Roberto peeks over and says, "She's here. Thanks." He waves his driver off, then, hooking his cane over his shoulder, puts a hand on each of the safety railings and, balancing his body in the air, swings forward and back and then side to side.

Now comes the real test, he thinks as he starts down the steps, all sixty of them. Kaede sits on a bench just beyond the end of the stairs, watching the great cascade of the falls. The rush and roar of the falling water masks the sounds of Roberto's approach, so it's not until he whispers her name, just before lightly kissing the back of her neck, that Kaede turns to face him.

"Roberto!" She stares at him. "You've given up your cast. And your crutch! And, oh dear. . . how did you get down here without help?"

"Riding on waves of virtue and fortitude," he replies. "It's a somewhat shaky vehicle for me, given that I'm not too used to it, but it's bringing me back to where I was as a child."

"Sit," says Kaede, standing in case he needs help.

It is an order Roberto gladly accepts, although one hand on his cane and one on the bench is all the help he needs. Kaede sits again, sliding close, and they embrace. It isn't until they separate some minutes later that Roberto notices the Buddha Amida's case lying under the bench.

How faithful she is to her father's admonition to keep the Buddha with her always! Does she take that statue everywhere she goes?

"I hope it wasn't too difficult for you to come out here, Roberto," she says, "but I had to talk to you right away. Your cover is so good no one in your office could, or in any case, no one *would*, over the telephone, tell me exactly where to find you. So I just gave them my password again and asked them to send you to our 'agreed upon emergency meeting place' as soon as possible.

"That did it, I guess, since here you are, but even so, it was a strange wait at first. I'd been here just a few minutes, when a big light blue car with some white writing I couldn't read on its doors, stopped up there, and someone got out and scoped me with field glasses. What especially got to me was that it happened so soon after I got here. Made me wonder if someone had been following me."

"I'm glad you told me about that, Kaede, but you can relax. I know that car, and that was one of our people, double-checking I guess, even though I told them it was okay when they gave me your message. Sorry they scared you, but it's nice to know how well they're doing their jobs. But now, speak to me, please. I'm eager to hear your message."

"Ok, but first let me have a little kiss on the other side of my neck to balance the last one. Mmm, good. And now, maybe another on the front of my face, to keep it from getting jealous. Mmm. *Mmm*. Better yet."

She straightens and makes a little space by sliding down the bench. "Now, back to business. Here's what I had to talk about. First and worst: I feel terrible having to do this so close to elections, but I have to go back to Tres Lagos right away. It's about Gétulio. He's terribly ill with cholera."

"That *is* serious. Especially for the young."

"Yes, and senhor Salles says that the poor little fellow constantly calls for me from his fever-dreams."

"Well then, of course you must go. At once. Your presence may be the most powerful medicine available to him."

"But will you be all right with all the pre-election things we have to do? There's *so* much stuff, and so *little* time to do it in. And I also wanted to be here to help you get around."

"Don't worry about what needs to get done, and don't worry about my getting around. We've got lots of volunteers waiting to help. Things won't go as smoothly without you here, but we'll get the most important things done in time, I'm sure.

"And as for helping me get around, you can see for yourself how I'm getting better. I came all the way from the parking lot to here by myself. And Candido, who is also doing much better, will be around to help me if I need it, as will my driver and others."

"Well, okay then. But here, take this envelope. It contains a list of pre-election tasks for your staff. I did talk with my assistant by telephone about most of the things on the list, but I forgot to mention a few details, so please give her a copy."

"I will. And next?"

"Well ..." she begins, then slips into a long silence.

While he waits for her to continue, Roberto's attention is diverted by the wonders of light and water that make up the constantly changing face of the cascades. And while he watches, he is treated to an especially wild display of nature, as a group of black vultures plunge from nearby trees and attach themselves, beak and claw, onto the carcass of a huge rodent. The rodent—a capybara almost as big as a man—crashes over the falls and drifts off into the shadows of the forest, with its company feasting aboard.

The show captivates Kaede as well, leaving the two of them staring at each other in silence, until Kaede says, "By the time I return from Tres Lagos, you'll no longer just be senhor Roberto, you'll be Senador Roberto."

"Perhaps."

"Perhaps? You're still unsure?"

"Well, yes, given that the central problem remains the same. We have too little money to ensure a proper count. If nothing big changes, the establishment will win, no matter what the actual vote. The only difference will be that post-election, the establishment will be able to claim—since they will be reported as the electoral victors—that their exercise of power now reflects the will of the people."

"So that's still the case, even after you informed the Marechal of their latest demands? You did inform him, didn't you?"

"I did, and he assured me once again that the army will do all it can to protect the vote. But though the army can control much of the actual voting by doing things like marking your identity card once you've voted, they're not trained enough or dispersed enough to control the actual counting. That is done by too many hands at too many levels, many of them free to report whatever they like.

"The Marechal still supports my plan to outbid the opposition at the last minute, but since we now know the size of the opposition's last offer, that plan is in total jeopardy now. Their current offer is a lot more money than we have or know how to get."

"So in today's Brasil, Roberto, vote counts are just commodities."

"You've got it. And like other commodities, their value is determined by demand, and the establishment has created a demand that we can't challenge."

"But what will happen when the false election results are announced? After all, the people will know they've been cheated. They talk, and they hear of the pre-election polls. How do you think they'll react?"

"I don't know, Kaede. Riots maybe, but I doubt it. And even if there are riots, far from reclaiming the election, riots would more likely antagonize the army. The army above all wants to maintain civil order, so in the face of riots it will either return the power to the establishment, or it will continue governing as yet another dictatorship. So at best, we'd get one dictatorship replacing another—something that all of us, including the Marechal, want to avoid."

Kaede stares silently ahead, gradually focusing on the emerging vision of the Buddha Amida. He rises from the vapors of the falls, settles on a bed of lotus blossoms floating cloudlike in the air, and says, *"It is time, Kaede. It is time for you to perform the act of kindness for which your father, the Buddha, has prepared you."*

His message delivered, the Buddha Amida ascends in the sky and vanishes from view.

Kaede stands, lifts the Buddha's case onto the bench, and says, "Here, Roberto, take the Buddha Amida and deliver him to senhor Carlos at *Vale de Oro, Praça Cinco de Maio en Rio* (Valley of Gold, Fifth of May Plaza, in Rio.) Tell senhor Carlos that this is the Buddha Amida whom senhor Salles discussed with him. Senhor Carlos is prepared to give you the money we'll need to outbid the opposition."

"But Kaede, we need *at least twelve million more than we have!* No gilt statue can be worth that much."

"The Buddha Amida, Roberto, is not gilt, but pure gold. And senhor Carlos, on a preliminary appraisal, told senhor Salles it should generate at least twenty-two million. Take what we need to ensure the count and ask senhor Carlos to keep the remainder in his safe. We can use it for other party needs, if need be."

"Oh, Kaede! How wonderful! But what about your promise to your father? Didn't he tell you to always keep the Buddha Amida with you?"

"Only so that it would be available 'to be of help to others.' That was his mission in his last life, and to sell it now, for this purpose, is perfectly in accord with that."

"Then this is what I'd like to do," Roberto says "After deducting what we need to ensure a legitimate count, we'll use the rest to support anti-establishment candidates other than the PDP's, according to their needs. Would that be all right?"

"Sounds perfect to me."

"Then I'm on my way." Roberto lifts the Buddha's case, slides the straps over a shoulder, and carefully stands, cane on one side, Kaede at the other.

"It's heavy, Roberto. Let me help you take it to your car."

"Thanks. It is heavy, but I can manage," he says, after taking a few experimental steps.

"Then good-bye, Roberto. I must run to Gétulio now. I'll catch a taxi in the visitor's lot, which should be opening soon. But I'll come back to you as soon as I can."

"No, wait, Kaede. Come with me. My driver and I will take you to the station."

"Oh, good! I get to spend a little more time with you."

Roberto takes a few more steps and says, "You know, Kaede, maybe I could use a little help with the Buddha Amida after all."

Sitting in his van after dropping Kaede off at the Omnibus Centro, Roberto opens the case in his lap and smiles what might be his greatest smile ever. As he peeks in the case, the Buddha Amida, in dazzling gold against white silk, benevolently returns his smile.

"Vale de Oro, Praça Cinco de Maio en Rio," Roberto says to his driver, "Pronto, por favor."

Masaru is dozing on the bench of his donkey cart at the intersection of the Camino Real and the road to Cafezal Tres Lagos, when he awakens to a familiar sound. He stretches and climbs down from his cart, moments before the omnibus clears the hill and pulls to a stop nearby.

As soon as the passenger door opens, Kaede steps out and finds herself face to face with Masaru, just inches away. They eye each other uncertainly for a moment, then they both twitch, jump forward, and hug.

"Masaru, my love!"

"Kaede, my Kaede!"

The driver carries Kaede's suitcase from the bus to the cart, salutes the couple, and starts to walk away. But Kaede catches his sleeve and tries to pass him a bill.

"Oh no, dona Kaede," he says. "Many thanks, but I cannot take money from you."

"No? Why not?"

"Oh, excuse me, dona Kaede, you not know me. I am Kyoami's brother, Ryoku. I come from Curitiba to help him farm when I not be driving omnibus. And Kyoami, he talk of many favors senhor Salles gives to him. He also say you are family of senhor Salles. This be why I cannot take money."

"I see. Well then, Ryoku, please accept my thanks instead, and give my best wishes to Kyoami."

"Thank you, dona Kaede. I do so today."

Kaede and the driver exchange little bows, but as soon as the driver steps back on the bus, Masaru raises a hand in an arresting motion. "Wait!" he says. "Do not go." As the driver waits, Masaru turns to Kaede. "Kaede, is not the Buddha Amida on the omnibus? Did you not bring it with you?"

"No. I have only a suitcase today."

"But the Buddha Amida is *always* with you, Kaede. Where is he today?"

"The Buddha, wherever he is, is exactly where he should be."

She does not want to tell me. Why? Where is Buddha Amida? Did she give Him to Roberto?

Kaede waves good-bye to the bus driver, and as the bus pulls away, she embraces Masaru again and whispers into his ear, "Masaru, dear, dear Masaru. Don't be so worried about losing me. I love you now, and I always will."

As they approach the portal arch fronting the last kilometer to the casa da cafezal, Masaru halts his cart to let senhor Salles's Bentley pass from the opposite direction. He lifts an arm to salute the senhor, but it is not senhor Salles riding in the passenger seat. It is but a flash of flaming red hair, blue-green eye shadow, and gold lamé cloth.

Minutes later, Masaru and Kaede arrive to see senhor Salles, ever alert to the sound of approaching hooves, standing in front of the casa. Kaede, too excited to wait for the donkey to stop, jumps from the cart and, with arms out wide, runs to senhor Salles. They hug and separate and hug again; and then, taking Kaede by the hand, senhor Salles leads her into the casa, explaining that Gétulio, though still feverish, is showing signs of recovery.

A few days later, Masaru is trimming shrubs in the garden while Kaede sits nearby on a rock at the edge of the koi pond, reading to Gétulio.

"And then," Kaede reads, "'the little mouse bit through the net and set its new friend free.'"

"I like the mouse," says Gétulio. "And I like the lion too."

"And how about the animals that live here on your father's plantation? Do you like them too?"

"Yes, I like them all, but I like the jaguar and the blue crowned pigeon best of all."

"Why is that?"

"I like the pigeon because it's so funny, with its feathers sticking out of its head. It looks like it's wearing a hat for Carnaval. And the jaguar is so beautiful. But he is hard to watch because he likes to hide. I only watched him once, when I was very little. I was with my papai and your papai and Kyoami. We hid behind some bushes and watched the jaguar catch a rabbit. But sometimes the jaguar scares me when he roars at night.

"Can we go look for the pigeon, dona Kaede? I heard him in the forest this morning. I know where he is."

Kaede laughs. She feels Gétulio's forehead. *Good. Still some fever, but less than yesterday.*

"Gétulio, I think you will grow up to be a biologist."

"What is a biologist?"

"A biologist is someone who loves plants and animals, and likes to look at them and learn all about them and take care of them."

"Yes, I want to be a biologist. But first I want to find the pigeon. Can we go look for him?"

"Soon. One day soon, we will look for him. But right now, it's time for you to have some lunch and take a nap. Later, when you are better, we will go into the forest, and you can help me find the pigeon."

"Oh, good!"

"But now, let's go see what dona Mercedes has made for us to eat." Kaede gathers Gétulio up, hangs him across her shoulders, and carries him to the casa, singing: "Potatoes! Potatoes! Who wants to buy a sack of potatoes?"

*

Kaede and Masaru, the remnants of a picnic before them, sit on a blanket at the edge of Lago Grande, watching a great willow swing in rhythm with the shifting breezes of an evening freshet.

Kaede fills two glasses with red wine—her first of the evening and Masaru's second. She passes a glass to Masaru and raises her own. "To our love."

Masaru extends his glass to join Kaede's, but he moves too quickly. The glasses clash, spilling wine onto the blanket. Masaru looks at the stain, shrugs, refills his glass, and downs it directly.

Kaede sips from her glass and then, after rocking the base of the glass in the sand to flatten a resting place for it, she leaves it there and, sighing in satisfaction, lies back on the blanket, facing the last of the setting sun.

"It's so beautiful, the sunset tonight," she says. "So many colors at once. It's so beautiful it's hard for me to look at. Does that happen to you, Masaru? Do you sometimes find certain things too beautiful to look at?"

"Yes," he says. "You are too beautiful to *only* look at." And with those words, he leans over, grasps her waist, pulls her roughly to him, and tears her blouse apart.

"No, no!" Kaede shouts, twisting and pushing to get loose. She manages to free herself, but Masaru lunges again, backhanding her mouth and wrestling her to the ground.

This time she does not shout, but stabs at both of his eyes, her fingers gathered into cones, all nails forward.

He rears back, screaming: "Monster witch!" Kaede breaks loose again and snatches up the bread knife. Standing, she assumes a threatening pose with the knife held before her. "No, Masaru. No!"

He backs off, moving out of her reach. He stares off into the distance for a minute, then turns to her with a wry smile on his face.

He's always been impulsive, she reminds herself, *and boys tend to be like that when sex is involved. But this is too much! Or did he misunderstand why*

I brought him out here? It was me who invited him and me who brought the wine. But wait, he does seem to be trying to calm down.

"You are like a tigress today," he says, in conversational tones. "I have never seen you like that before. Why did you fight me?"

"That was too soon, Masaru. You must wait for me to tell you I'm ready. But until then, you must be gentle. It's too soon for us to do what you want to do."

"Too soon, too soon. You must be gentle and you must wait," he parrots in a mocking tone, as a growing rage distorts his features. "Masaru already knows about waiting for you," he says. "Masaru always waits, always waits, and waits, for you."

He grabs the wine bottle, swallows the wine that is left, and then spins away and marches to the lake. Facing the lake, his back to Kaede, he stands motionless for a while. Then he grunts, turns around, and starts walking back toward her.

What now? she wonders.

Drawing near, Masaru slows his pace and drops into a crouch, the sort she last saw when they used to play Lion and Lamb as children.

Still standing, Kaede grabs the empty wine bottle and spreads her legs to brace herself. Raising the bottle in one hand and the bread knife in the other, she calmly says: "All right, Masaru, now it's me who's waiting. I'm waiting for you to come one step closer, and then I will end your waiting for you, once and for all."

Masaru has never really known physical fear, and were Kaede a man, even a stronger man than he, he would not hesitate to try to take the knife and kill the other man. But now he does feel fear. It's not that he's afraid of what Kaede might do to him. He knows he could disarm her—but what he fears is that disarming her might mean killing her.

Kill Kaede? He doesn't have time to reason it out, but his heart knows that to kill Kaede would be to kill himself. There is only one thing left for him to do, and he does it. He turns and slowly walks off, finds a suitable spot far on the other side of the lake, and assumes the lotus position.

The sun has slipped beneath the horizon, yielding the sky to twilight, by the time Masaru, largely calmed, walks back along the lakeshore. Kaede has fallen asleep, and as he looks at her, he thinks of the time, years ago, when he almost entered her private parts. *Does she still have her virgin's veil?* he wonders, once again. *No, it cannot be. Roberto must have taken it by now. But maybe not. If she makes me wait, maybe she also makes him wait. Maybe she wants us to wait because she wants to keep it for marriage. And she is a strong woman. So maybe the veil will still be mine. And, as my father said: "He who takes the veil has the key to the lock." So maybe …*

She is so beautiful asleep. I could … But no. If I take her now, she will run away to Roberto. So I will wait. I will wait, just as she says I must.

From a distant hill, Kyoami, returning home from market late, sees Kaede and Masaru walking hand in hand on a hill, silhouetted by the moonlight. He sees them stop and embrace, but then a deep bank of clouds spreads over the moon, covering the couple with darkness.

The next morning, with the skirt of her chiffon nightgown drawing her into the breeze, Kaede steps through her bedroom door into the glow of a sun so perfectly matched in hue to the blue of the sky that the whole of the view seems but an idealized artist's composition. But her mind will not let her dwell on the view.

What should I do, she asks herself. *Masaru is so dangerous when he's angry, and so perfect when he's calm. When he's calm, he just takes life moment by moment, always doing his best, never worrying about the future like I do. If only the anger didn't come along with the calm.*

Last night I went from loving him to hating him to loving him again. Will he always check his rage? Last night it already went much too far. What would keep it from going further? Nothing. As grows his want of me, so grows his fear of losing me, and as grows his fear, so grows his rage.

But losing Masaru is also a fear of my heart, a fear perhaps as great as my fear of him. So what can I do? If I stay, he will assault me again, and then? And then?

I really have no choice. I must banish Masaru from both my heart and my mind and go to Roberto instead. Roberto will love me and protect me, and as my love for Roberto grows, my love for Masaru will diminish.

Go to Roberto, Kaede. *That is what you must do!*

A knock at the door announces dona Mercedes. She is shocked by Kaede's swollen lips and her red, sleep-deprived eyes, but maintains her discretion and asks only whether Kaede needs any help.

"No, thank you, I'm all right," says Kaede. "I just fell in the underbrush on a late night walk."

"Then may I bring you breakfast?"

"No, thank you. I'm not hungry yet."

"All right," says dona Mercedes, "but I have to leave for market now. You'll find water for your coffee on the warm edge of the stove, and fresh croissants in the bread box."

"Thank you, dona Mercedes."

On a warm afternoon some days later, Kaede is driving a pony cart along a field trail with Gétulio beside her. Gétulio, though recovering, still looks wan and, being prone to fits of shivering, is wrapped in a woolen blanket. "I'm too hot," he says.

Kaede stops the cart and loosens the blanket, but leaves it draped over his shoulders. "Let's leave it this way, so you can just pull it around you if the chills come back."

Approaching a pair of workers—a man and a woman—carrying newly harvested coffee beans on their heads in large, flat baskets, Kaede slows the cart and stops alongside.

The workers put their baskets down and, after an exchange of greetings, the woman asks, "How are you feeling today, Gétulio?"

"Better, senhora, much better. Thank you."

The woman smiles at the news and, touching the primitive wooden cross that hangs from her neck on a leather cord, she faces Kaede. Lifting an inquiring eyebrow, she tilts her head toward Gétulio.

Kaede nods assent, and the woman slips the cross and cord from her neck and offers it to Gétulio, who eagerly extends his neck.

As she hangs the cross on Gétulio, the woman says, "Take my cross, little Gétulio. It has been blessed by a *padre santo,* who promised it will forever grant the prayers of the one who wears it, if he prays with care and love. So hold it close when you pray, and you will soon be well."

Next, the man addresses Gétulio, saying: "On the night of the full moon, I will write your name in the earth and leave a bottle of the finest pinga and cigars at the crossing of the trails where *O Querreiro*, the White Warrior and his lover meet. And O Querreiro and his lover will drink the pinga and smoke the cigars and will be happy. And they will see your name and will thank you for the gifts by banishing the evil spirit that visits you."

"Thank you, senhor," says Gétulio, wide-eyed with delight. Then, grimacing in pain, he turns to Kaede and urgently points at his stomach. Kaede gathers him in an arm, picks up a satchel and towel from the cart and, saying good-bye to the workers over her shoulder, hurries him into the field.

Later that day, with Gétulio soundly napping under the watchful eye of dona Mercedes, Kaede approaches the Japanese garden on a walk with dona Elsa.

Masaru is lacquering a part of the pagoda that was scarred by a falling tree limb, and for a moment, Kaede considers taking a detour. *No,* she tells herself. *I'll not let fear of Masaru determine my actions. If he embarrasses me before dona Elsa, so be it. But if he speaks first, and in a civil tongue, I will reply in like manner.*

But Masaru turns his back as the women approach, and they pass by without exchange.

He's still angry that I didn't let him come visit me in to my bedroom last night. Can he really think that the simple passage of a few days would make everything all right between us? How bizarrely optimistic! But then, that's always been Masaru.

Kaede is rowing a skiff on Lago Grande with Gétulio in front, when they approach a pair of swans herding a trio of cygnets before them.

"Look, dona Kaede!" Gétulio shouts. "Swans with babies. Let's go close. Let's go close. I want to catch a baby!"

Kaede laughs. "Let's just watch them, Gétulio. We can go a little closer, but if we get too close, the father swan will peck us hard with his very strong beak."

Carefully keeping their distance to just beyond where the male starts making warning noises, Kaede and Gétulio follow the swans until they arrive at a shallow place. There the birds feed on water lily tubers until, finished with lunch, they herd their cygnets before them while swimming with one foot in the air.

Gétulio is amazed. He's never seen swans swimming up close before.

In answer to his question, Kaede tells him that swimming with one foot in the air allows them to dry their feet even as they swim, adding that, "It keeps their skin from getting all wrinkled up like ours does if we take too long a bath."

"But, but ... Oh, I see. Now they're switching feet, so both feet can get dry. I thought maybe only one foot got to dry."

Kaede smiles at the expression on Gétulio's face. She knows that just as soon as he learns to swim, he's going to try that one-legged trick himself.

Later, having rowed out of view of the swans, Gétulio and Kaede approach a tiny island covered with a multitude of swan feathers—most small, some large, and a few enormous. Anticipating Gétulio's next question, Kaede explains that the island is where the swans come to pick and clean themselves, and to get rid of old, used-up feathers to make room for new ones.

Gétulio, grinning over an idea, startles Kaede by jumping from the skiff onto the island. Wobbling around on the island's boggy surface, he gathers a large number of feathers, stuffing them into his shirt.

"What are you going to do with those?" asks Kaede.

"I'm going to make uh, uh . . . a bouquet."

"A bouquet?

"Yes. A bouquet. No, two bouquets. No, *three* of them."

"And what are you going to do with three bouquets?"

"I'm going to give one to dona Mercedes, and one to dona Elsa, and one to you, dona Kaede. But, oh bah! Now I can't surprise you."

*

Over the following week, Gétulio's fever disappears, his eyes regain their sparkle, and Dr. Antonio pronounces him cured.

11

One Finger, More or Less?

Senhor Salles is in his library, half-dozing while delighting in the scent of his favorite leather chair, when barely audible words coming from his radio rouse him. He increases the volume and hears:

> "And I repeat: With almost 90 percent of the votes counted, it appears that senhor Roberto Millefiore has—in a historical first for the newly legitimized Partida Democratica Popular—been elected Senador for O Estado do São Paolo. Not long ago, Senador elect Millefiore was a political prisoner, and now he is an elected representative of the people. How quickly Brasil can change its vests!"

Senhor Salles jumps up, goes to the door, and calls for Kaede. But it is dona Mercedes who appears, feather duster in hand, saying: "Dona Kaede told me about an hour ago that she was going for her daily walk by the lakes, senhor."

"Please find her and ask her to come here at once. Tell her that *most important* news concerning the elections is being broadcast on the radio."

Minutes later, Kaede, her eyes wide and round with anticipation, rushes into the room.

"Ah, Kaede," senhor Salles says, *"A novidades maravilhoso! Roberto foi eleitado!* (Marvelous news! Roberto has been elected!)"

Happiness blazes from Kaede's face as she takes senhor Salles by both hands, pulls him from his chair, and waltzes him around the room.

Such wonderful youthful vitality, he thinks. *And her fragrance! How fabulous it would be to awaken in its aura each day!*

The next morning Kaede, wrapped in a loose-knit shawl, sits on her patio savoring the crispness of the morning air while listening to the territorial cheep of a finch.

He sounds really close, so why can't I find him? I've looked everywhere. Oh, there he is. Bravo, Mr. Finch. How perfectly camouflaged.

His golden wings held loose, the finch, perched within a corona of golden blossoms, is just one more petal among the many on the giant hibiscus.

Leaning back in her chaise, eyes closed, Kaede is considering her options for a wake-up walk, when a different song commands her attention. It is the plaintive song of Roberto's ancient Citroen, complaining, in its old age, of the steepness of the incline.

Jumping up from her chair, Kaede runs through the house and meets Roberto in the driveway, shouting: "Roberto Senador! Roberto Senador! Bravo o Senador!"

They hug and kiss and start to prance about, when Kaede suddenly stops and exclaims, "Roberto, you are recovered. You're jumping up and down, and you're not even using your cane."

"*Almost* recovered," he says. "I'm limping yet, and wearing a hidden brace, but yes, I'm nearly healed."

She takes Roberto's hand and leads him down a trail, heading for a favorite flowered grove. Both too blissful to feel the fiery gaze that follows them, they settle on a huge fallen log, carved into a bench shape by Masaru. Kaede rests her head on Roberto's lap, from where, already in a high state of happiness, she thrills to the beauty of the wild clematis that decorate the canopy above.

Birds and flowers and vines, and best of all, the touch of Roberto. It's hard to imagine a more perfect morning than the present. I can't remember one.

Kaede's search of her memory for a comparably wonderful day is interrupted by Roberto, who says, in a voice of controlled excitement: "Oh, by the way, Kaede, I've found the perfect house in Rio. It's near the senate and close to the ocean, both. And it has two beautiful gardens, one inside and one outside, and a lovely casinha for our housekeeper."

Did he say "our"? Did he really mean to say our *housekeeper, his and mine, or did he just mean* a *housekeeper? I'd better listen carefully here.*

"Oh, Roberto, that sounds expensive. Will you be able to afford it?"

"Yes, I think so. Senatorial salaries haven't yet been specified, but the Marechal has mentioned a generous target figure. A figure in line with his publicly stated belief that elected officials should be well paid, if for no other reason than to reduce government corruption. And after all, it's the Marechal and his junta cohort who will determine what salaries will be—at least at first."

"How wonderful! So many good things are happening at once."

"Yes, it is wonderful to realize that the people are finally going to have a voice in their futures. And that is ultimately due to your generosity, Kaede."

"Due ultimately to the vigorous and brave campaigning of you and others, you might better say."

"I was referring to your rescuing the people's votes with your gift of the Buddha Amida."

"Well, even that was about my father's generosity, not mine."

"All right, let me amend that. Due to the generosity of both your father and yourself.

"But here, lest I forget, here's a small present for you."

Kaede opens the tiny velvet-covered box Roberto passes her, and in a voice turned to song by delight, she says, "Oh Roberto, it's so beautiful. How perfect! A red tourmaline surrounded by four green emeralds. Tourmalines are my birthstone, you know, and the red ones—they're so rare—are my favorites. How did you know?"

"Just intuition. It seemed the right stone for you." *No need to tell her about her girlfriend telling me.*

"Oh, it's so beautiful, Roberto. It's almost too grand to accept. I can't even think of the right words to thank you!"

"Let me see if I can suggest some words. Umm, what if you were to say, Roberto, yes, I'll marry you?"

Kaede is on the verge of repeating Roberto's last words, when a picture rises from a foggy area of her mind. She pauses. *Devil, go!* she silently commands. *Go, devil, go!*

But Masaru's face, intense black eyes aglow, is slow to fade, and even when she manages to erase it, she is left a shaken woman, with her head in her hands.

Roberto waits.

Looking up, Kaede says, "How can I say this, Roberto? I do love you and I do want to marry you, but something deep inside me is holding me back. I won't say no, but I can't say yes. Can you give me a little more time to conquer my confusion?" *Oh, Kaede, is that all you can do anymore, is ask everyone to wait?*

Roberto, his voice revealing his pain at her rejection, despite his effort to hide it, says, "Of course you can ask me to wait. I knew you might not be ready."

I probably shouldn't tell her that senhor Salles told me about Masaru's proposal. "But tell me, if you will, is your hesitation about your feelings for Masaru or your feelings for me? You told me a long while ago that he was your first love. So I'm wondering if you love him still?"

"Yes, my hesitation is partly about Masaru, and though I don't love him as I did, and though I do love you, there's still … I—I don't know. I can't answer your question just now."

"Then don't. I'll wait. I'll wait for you for as long as you tell me there is still a chance."

"Oh yes! There's a chance. There's more than a chance, Roberto, there is! It's just that …"

He wraps his arms around her shoulders and kisses her. It is a loving kiss, though restrained. She kisses him back passionately and he quickly responds in kind. Then they lie next to each other, there on the log, loosely entangled, until a light drizzle sits them up.

Returning the ring to the box, Kaede offers it back to Roberto.

"Oh no, please keep it," he says. "Please. I want you to keep it no matter what. But here's an idea. Why don't you wear it on your right hand and see if it doesn't magically find its way to your left?"

"Thank you, Roberto dear. I will wear it proudly, but not on my right hand. I'll keep my right hand for my friend's jade ring, and I'll wear yours on the second finger of my left hand. That way it won't have as far to go to get to where I want it. And in the meantime, when I'm asked where I got such a beautiful ring—which is sure to happen a lot—I will say that it was a present from the most perfect man I know!"

Leaving the grove, they stroll to the edge of the lake where, standing under a great conifer, they watch the light rain sparkle the lake and bring glisten to the flora.

Arriving back at the casa, Roberto says, "I hate to have to leave you so soon, Kaede, but I must return to Rio. There are so many things I must do before the senate's first meeting."

"I understand that, of course," she says, "but why go back right now? It'll be late and dark, and you'll be too tired to work by the time you get there. Wouldn't you rather spend the night with me and leave, rested, after breakfast in the morning?"

"You're inviting me to spend the night with *you?*"

"Yes."

"Oh, Kaede, of course I would rather! I could never turn down such an offer. But won't senhor Salles, well-known Catholic that he is, object to my staying with you?"

"Senhor Salles, however Catholic he may be, has always respected my right to make my choices as I will. Besides, he is much too intelligent to be demonized by the fears of a celibate clergy. Please stay, Roberto. It may help me find my way."

"Then yes, of course I'll stay."

"Wonderful!" she says, and folds her body into his.

The next morning, Kaede and Roberto eat breakfast with senhor Salles, an experience the men relish as an opportunity to get to know each other a little better.

*

A few days later, Kaede and senhor Salles are picking their way down an animal path in the tract of dense, wild jungle that he lets grow between two of the lakes, when he says, "Thank you for accompanying me, Kaede. But I must confess that the reason I asked you to come along is not primarily to search for the wild orchid I mentioned—though I do hope we find it. Actually I need to speak to you of a more serious matter."

"And what could be more serious than finding a wild orchid?"

"I do love your humor, dear lady, but I want you to know that I have been informed by a friend, a captain of Federales, that an attempt was made on the life of Senador Roberto. An attempt in which you also were wounded."

"Well yes, there was an attack, and Roberto was seriously hurt, though he's nearly recovered. My wound, however, happened at a different time, and was accidental and trivial. Look here, see this tiny little scar? That's the only residual."

"I see. Well, I am glad for that. But still, as you know, I consider you my daughter, and I need to feel that I'm protecting you as well as a father can. So I want you to give me your word that, in the future, you will report any attack or threat involving you or Roberto to me at once. Even if it seems trivial at the time."

"I'm moved by your wish to protect me, and I will report any future attack or threat to you at once, as you wish. Though, thankfully, I don't think there's much risk anymore, not now that the election results are in and have been accepted by the junta."

"Thank you for the promise, Kaede. But I must also tell you that my friend considers you and Roberto, both of you, to be still at risk."

"Still?"

"So says my friend, and he is surely in a position to know."

"I hope your friend is just being overly cautious, but, of course, I'll do whatever I can to reduce the risk. Tell me what to do."

"Well, apart from the obvious security protections, which my friend will pass on to you when he visits for dinner tomorrow—You will be here, won't you?"

"Yes, I'll be here."

"Then, for now, the one particular thing I would like to suggest is … is so self-serving that I hesitate to say it."

"Oh, senhor, do tell me, whether it seems self-serving or not. Self-serving is a proper way to be, as long as it is not at the cost of others. And I know you much too well to worry about that."

"Well, as you know, along with Cafezal Tres Lagos, I inherited certain connections—some of which date back to the regency of Pedro II—among those lineages who have for many years been governing Brasil. And those connections make me part of an alliance that will retain much of its power even under an elected government, since it's based on property and wealth and the control of much of the country's employment,"

"But this alliance feels threatened by democracy?"

"Yes. Not all of them, of course. There are a number of us who want to share what we have with those less fortunate. But there are also others who habitually meet threats, imagined or real, with force. These, of course, are the dangerous ones.

"However, it's also true that all members of the alliance are controlled by a strict code of honor that mandates that they support and protect one another. And it is that mandate that I believe we could use to protect both you and Roberto."

"How so, senhor?"

"Well, as I said, my proposal is highly self-serving, and I'm still afraid that stating it will diminish your respect for me."

"Please tell me, senhor Salles. The depth of our friendship is such that I am sure nothing you might say will diminish my respect or love for you."

"Yes, then all right. Because of the code of honor, if you were my wife, you would at once become highly protected, and I could adopt Roberto as well, which would gain him the same protection. It would be unusual, but no one would object, as to do so would be to question the canon of the alliance."

"Senhor Salles, you are offering to *marry* me to protect me!"

"Yes, there's that, and also to gain a wonderful mother for Gétulio. And, if you can forgive the fantasies of an aging man, not least of all, to acquire you as my lover."

Kaede is silent as they slowly continue down the path. She wholeheartedly wants to please senhor Salles, but she has thought of him as her surrogate father for so long that the notion of becoming his lover seems nearly incestuous. *There's no way I could,* she thinks. *But aha, look at me: He and Roberto and Masaru make three.*

She laughs sharply at the absurdity of her situation and, as if in response to her laughter, a large deer emerges from the underbrush, springs explosively across their path and sprays them with sand as it crashes into the forest and disappears from view.

Though momentarily frightened by the deer, they brush sand from their clothes and, the tension broken, senhor Salles says, "Please excuse me, Kaede, if I have upset you unnecessarily. I apologize."

"I'm not upset by what you said, senhor Salles. On the contrary, I'm most moved by the love and trust implicit in your offer, but I must decline."

"I understand, and I respect your decision. Still, it was thoughtless of me to have expressed my wish to have you as a lover, especially since I know you have slept with Roberto. I'm afraid I was so prepossessed by my own selfish hopes, I overlooked the obvious: Your heart is with Roberto."

"Yes, my heart is with Roberto, though unfortunately, not *only* with Roberto."

"Ah, yes, the other, Masaru. I do recall your telling me, as we rode to your graduation, that he had asked for your hand."

"Yes, it is Masaru. I'm still stuck over him, though my feelings for him are such that they make me question my own sanity. Sometimes I feel I will die if I go to him, and sometimes I feel I will die if I don't. And those feelings coexist with the more rational conviction—and it really *is* a conviction—that I should go to Roberto. To Roberto the pure, to Roberto the open, to Roberto the loving, whom I love in turn, and who has also asked for my hand."

She holds up her ring for senhor Salles to see.

"Then let me withdraw my offer to marry you," he says, "and let me instead advise you as a father might. You must, of course, do as your heart demands, but I think that Masaru, though I love him like a son, is of a temperament far too volatile and far too anchored in archaic tradition for a free spirit like you to marry.

"Go not to Masaru, I would say, but to Roberto. Though I do not know him well, I am told is an honest man of kindly disposition. Further, if you marry Roberto here at Cafezal Tres Lagos, I will invite the ruling cohort to attend the ceremony. And, if you allow me to give the bride away, you will be considered as if you were my daughter, and Roberto will be considered as if my son-in-law.

"In that way, you would both acquire the protection you need, and I, in the meantime, will do what I can to comfort Masaru."

"Senhor Salles, your advice is clearly born of generosity and divination. It is to Roberto that I must go, and still, and still— But no, no more stills! I will follow your advice, which is also the advice of my heart. I will go to Roberto and accept his offer, and I will ask you to give me over to him, and I will ever remain the grateful daughter of both yourself and my father."

"Good! I am indescribably pleased, Kaede. Will you want the wedding to take place soon?"

"Yes, I think so. I'm sure Roberto would like it to be soon, and now so do I, if for no other reason than to keep myself from vacillating any longer."

She puts her arms around senhor Salles and holds him in a bouquet of such innocence and love, that the carnal wishes that moments before had felt so urgent to him, vanish without a trace.

Walking back to the casa, senhor Salles asks Kaede when she will inform Roberto of her decision.

"Today, if I can reach him. I have the name of his hotel in Rio, where he is negotiating a house for us."

"The telephones are probably still out because of yesterday's storm, says senhor Salles, but if necessary, we can send a shortwave to a friend in Rio who will have it carried to Roberto."

The message Kaede sends is:

Roberto,

Wherever did you find my beautiful Mexican jumping ring? It has already leapt from my second finger, left hand, to my third finger, left hand. Come to me, my treasure, and let us grow our love in all the ways that we can imagine.

Your bride in waiting,

Kaede

It is early morning, crisp for the time of year in the tropic of Capricorn, but the light is bright, and the air is filled with the song and show of many birds, when Gétulio and Kaede paddle their canoe back to the pier on Lago Grande.

Senhor Salles catches the tie rope Gétulio throws, secures it to a hook on the pier, ties the second rope that Kaede tosses and, complimenting him on the accuracy of his throw, scoops Gétulio from his seat.

Climbing from the boat, Kaede says, "Gétulio wants to learn to swim, and he says that as soon as he does, he will teach me to swim as well, so that we can swim together. I also would like to learn to swim, especially with Gétulio as my teacher."

"Yes, Papai, and then I will become friends with the fish. Dona Kaede said so!"

"Ah, well, Gétulio, I certainly approve of your desires. It will be good for you to learn to swim, and it is certainly important to befriend one's fish. I will go to Aruja today and search for a teacher for you."

"Any word from Roberto?" Kaede asks.

"No, not yet," says senhor Salles.

12

A Message from Rio

About midmorning of the second day of waiting for a response from Roberto, Kaede is listlessly looking for something to read, when the whirr of an unfamiliar motor brings her to a library window. She sees a young man slide his motorcycle to a halt, leap from the seat, jerk the cycle onto its stand, and run to the front door.

The rider bangs repeatedly on the door until dona Mercedes, frowning at the young man's impudence, greets him with an annoyed, "Good morning! What is it?"

"Good morning, senhora. Is dona Kaede at home?"

"That depends. Who wants to know?"

"Excuse me," says the young man, eyes bulging and voice choking. "I'm Carlos Marinho from the PDP. I have urgent news for dona Kaede Miroka. It concerns Senador Millefiore."

"One moment, please."

The young man fidgets in place, turns around, and then turns back to find Kaede standing in the doorway. Her smile of greeting disappears the moment she sees his expression.

"Good morning. I am Kaede Miroka."

Carlos, struggling for words, glances at Kaede, looks off, studies the floor; and finally, with tears welling in his eyes, takes her hands in his and says, "Excuse me, dona Kaede. I'm Carlos Marinho from the PDS. I am so sorry, but—but I must inform you that Senador Roberto ... Roberto was assassinated ... last night in Rio."

Kaede screams: "Não! Não! Não!" and faints into Carlos's arms.

*

Kaede tosses in her bed as she dreams. She and Roberto are canoeing on Lago Grande, she in front, facing Roberto, who paddles from the rear. She looks down at the baby she's holding to her bosom and says, "He is so beautiful, Roberto, but can we be sure he's ours?"

"Of course he's ours. How could he not be? I planted the seed, and you brought it to fruition. Don't you remember?"

"Well, yes, I remember you planting the seed. It was wonderful. But I don't remember the rest. Shouldn't I remember carrying him? And shouldn't I remember giving birth to him?"

"It sure seems like you should, but I don't know. They say that sometimes people immediately forget events of great emotional importance. Maybe that's it. But look at his eyes. That should end your doubts. Look at his eyes! Who else's could he be but ours?"

Kaede holds the baby at arm's length and studies his eyes. "You're right," she says. "His eyes are exactly the shape of yours, though not quite the color of mine. But then babies almost always have a light eye color that changes as they get older. In any case, you are right, he has to be ours. But I still wish I could remember delivering him."

A cold wind blows across the lake, and Kaede wraps her shawl around the baby as Roberto turns the canoe in the direction of the pier. But even as he turns, the wind blows in a series of gusts, and waves begin to pitch and turn the boat. Roberto paddles as hard as he can, but the wind keeps shifting, and the boat begins to spin and dip, taking in water front and rear, and splashing Kaede and the baby. Holding the baby close, Kaede joins him as he whimpers.

The wind blows harder and harder, and the canoe rocks ever faster until it flips over, dumping its passengers into the water. Desperately treading water to simply stay afloat, Kaede holds the baby up in the air and screams: "Help! Help! Save the baby! I can't swim!"

Kaede wakes to find dona Elsa lying beside her, caressing Kaede's brow while purring soft sounds into her ear. Later, as Kaede calms, dona Elsa gently removes the pillow Kaede has been holding tightly to her breasts, and they lie together until Kaede drifts back to sleep. Then dona Elsa, after carefully tucking Kaede in, returns to her own bed, again leaving both their doors ajar.

Dona Elsa listens for a long while and, hearing no sound from Kaede's room, she goes back to sleep and soon is lightly snoring, giving Kaede the sign she's been waiting for. Kaede leaves the casa for the fields where, as a slim dark figure afloat in a gown, she disappears beneath the face of the moon.

Senhor Salles, dona Mercedes, dona Elsa, and Dr. Hermes gather in the main hallway, far from Kaede's bedroom.

"She will sleep now with the soporific I gave her," Dr. Hermes says as he hands a small package to dona Mercedes. "And here is more for later. The note attached tells the dosage, in case you forget. Start with three drops in a cup of warm milk at bedtime. Repeat if she is still awake in an hour, but do not exceed six drops per day.

"After two days, try just warm milk without telling her of the change, but don't hesitate to resume the medication if she fails to get to sleep in her usual time. Call me in ten days if she still requires medication to sleep."

"And what about her cuts and scratches?" senhor Salles asks.

"They are all superficial, Pedro, mostly berry bush scratches. Just keep them clean, and they should be all right. Use the tincture of iodine if any of the wounds fail to scab over or if you see any signs of pus. And now, if you will excuse me, I have to leave. But be sure to contact me over any further concerns."

"I will see you to your car, Antonio."

In the days that follow, Kaede wanders about like a vacant person. She smiles and speaks robotically, even to senhor Salles and Masaru. She walks the coffee fields by day, but is unresponsive to, and usually unaware of, the greetings of people she encounters.

Then late one night, dona Elsa, who in shifts with dona Mercedes, is keeping track of Kaede, finds Kaede's bedroom empty and the door to her patio open. She is not on the patio, and after a quick search of the casa yields no sign of her, dona Elsa rouses senhor Salles. Together with Masaru and several workers, he immediately begins a search of the grounds.

They start, on senhor Salles's hunch, with the Japanese garden, and find her in the pagoda, sitting in the lotus position. Her fingers form the peace mudra as she whispers prayers to Kuan Yin, asking for her compassionate blessings.

Senhor Salles sends the others home and waits outside the pagoda until, hours later, Kaede ends her prayers. He then takes her hand and leads her back to bed, where she promptly falls into a deep sleep.

*

Some days later Kaede, no longer the hollow-eyed essence of *tristesse*, is in the library, silently facing senhor Salles across a small table, when dona Mercedes enters the room. She puts a pot of coffee and a plate of pastries on the table, and asks if she can bring anything else. Senhor Salles shakes his head, and dona Mercedes leaves the room.

Turning back to Kaede, senhor Salles says, "I'm delighted that you are feeling well enough to join me now. It was not clear to me when I met you this afternoon just how well you felt."

"I only needed a little more rest, senhor."

"Good. That is what Antonio thought, that time and rest would heal you. He left us feeling almost at peace about you, but it has been difficult, seeing you present in person but gone in spirit."

"I am forever thankful for your patience, senhor. It's profoundly kind of you to support me as you do. But tell me, please, as strange as it may sound; how long was I spiritually gone?"

"For over a week, spiritually, and several days physically as well. The last time, two nights ago, was particularly unnerving. After a long search, we finally found you in a little gully hidden under some shrubbery. Twice we passed you by without notice, dogs and all.

"It was dona Elsa who at last came upon you, after hearing some small sounds you were making. You were incoherent and barely able to talk, but you revived quickly after drinking a quantity of water, which Dr. Hermes said was your most urgent need."

"You clearly have saved my life, at least once, senhor. I will never by able to repay you."

"Please don't talk that way, Kaede. It is payment enough for all of us who know and love you, to see you recovering."

"Senhor Salles, you are a bodhisattva of the highest order—if such an appellation does not conflict with your Catholicism. In which case you must be a seraphim, or whatever is the highest order of angel."

"You blaspheme the angels, dear child. But they, like I, can but love you nonetheless."

They touch coffee cups, then senhor Salles cranks up his Victrola, and they sink into their big chairs and ride to the rhythms of the *Cantos* of Pachelbel.

Kaede waits a while after the end of the music, and then, her eyes and voice projecting a single plea, she says, "I don't wish to sully a blessed moment, senhor, but I still must ask, trusting your kindness to allow it. Have you heard any more about Roberto's death?"

"Of course you must ask, Kaede. It is important for you to resolve such questions as fully as possible, and it is important to me as well. But, unfortunately, I have heard very little. I have asked the leaders of his party, who know nothing but what the police have told them. I have asked the police themselves, who reply that they know where and when his body was found, the approximate time of his death, and the caliber of the bullets that killed him, but nothing more."

"Nothing more! How can that be? Have they made any effort? Surely they should be able to discover who the murderer is! But oh, I'm sorry, senhor. Please forgive me. I've been shouting at you, you who seek only to comfort me."

"It is all right for you to shout, Kaede. Sometimes one *must* shout. But as regards the police, it is not surprising that they have little to offer, considering their general level of intelligence, their training and pay, and the extent of their corruption. They claim to be vigorously investigating the case, but I do not believe them. And, of course, it is common enough for the police themselves to operate as assassins."

"Then is that all we are to learn? Just that Roberto is gone? Is there nothing to be done? *Is there no justice to be had?*"

"Ah, justice: The plea of the poor and the fear of the rich. Lady Justice must reside somewhere in the land, perhaps in a cave deep in Amazonas, but how does one know where to look?"

Silence ensues as Kaede, a bit perplexed, stares at senhor Salles with an inquisitive expression. He coughs to clear a constriction born of embarrassment, and says: Now it's my turn to ask to be excused, Kaede. I spoke of justice metaphorically, as if in jest, while you are suffering personally."

"It's all right, senhor. I know that justice is hard to achieve in this land. *But this time we must have it!* This is not only about Roberto, it is about Brasil and its future. It is about what kind of a life Gétulio and the other children of his generation will have. It is about the freedom to be oneself, about being able to choose how to live your life!"

"What you say is true, Kaede, and I admire the passion of your beliefs, but —"

"Please! Oh please, senhor Salles. Can't you do something? *Won't* you do something? Won't you use the power you have to find the guilty and see to his punishment?

"If you will do that, I'll repay you in any way you wish. I'll become your wife. I'll become Gétulio's mother. I'll become your mistress. Whatever you want of me will be yours for the taking." Kaede slips to the floor on her knees, sobbing.

After resting a comforting hand on her shoulder and waiting for her to her calm a bit, senhor Salles picks Kaede up and carries her to a couch. There he holds her, tenderly stroking the back of her head until her weeping stops. Then he says, "Kaede, you are right. I should and I will do all that I can to gain justice for Roberto. It will benefit you, it will benefit me, and it will benefit the public to see that justice can be had. I will begin by speaking with my friend in the Federales."

Kaede places an arm around senhor Salles, lays her head on his shoulder, and thanks him several times in a tiny, childlike voice.

13

Friends Help Friends

Senhor Salles sits before a desk bearing a brass plaque inscribed: **CAPITÁO BARRACO** and studies the room. Behind the desk, a Brasilian flag hangs from a stand. On the wall to the right of the flag is a large, framed photograph of an Italian soccer team, whose leader holds aloft the golden medal of Olympic victory as Hitler and Mussolini salute from a stand.

The office door suddenly swings open. Shouting, "Pedroso! Pedroso!" Capitão Barraco rushes to his friend. They heartily embrace and, after studying his friend at arm's length, senhor Salles points to the picture on the wall and says, "João, you look just as young and fit now as you did back then in '36."

The captain laughs. He pinches a small roll of fat at his waist, purses his lips in doubt, and says, "Well, not *quite* as young and fit, but I do feel well. And you, my friend, you have never looked better!"

"Thank you, João. By the grace of God, I continue, despite advancing age and licentious habits, to be blessed with good health."

"And at the cafezal? All goes well?"

"Yes, very well. You must come and see."

"I will. I promise I soon will. I miss the beauty of the countryside that we used to roam. I will come and I will bring my falcons and we will ride your fields on horseback and hunt the skies. But for now, let us speak of the reason for your visit. You said, during our repeatedly disconnected call, that you were anxious to know more of the circumstances surrounding the death of Senador elect Millefiore."

"Yes, that is the main part of my mission—a mission I'm undertaking on behalf of a beloved."

"Hmm. Unfortunately, Pedroso, I have little to report right now, and the few official observations are already known to you. Beyond that, I have heard only rumors of uncertain veracity."

"I hoped you might have more."

"And perhaps we shall, Pedroso, but the situation is difficult. You seek information. I seek information. Even Marechal General Cruzado seeks information. But so far, we have found very little. All of which suggests that we are dealing with a planned and concealed, rather than a spontaneous, act."

"And the Policia Estadual? Do they know more than they have reported?"

"The Policia Estadual, I am convinced, know much more than they have reported, even though they insist they don't."

"But, João, there must be some way to find out what they *really* know."

"Well, of course, Pedroso. As you and I both well know, in Brasil there is always a way, especially if one supplies the right kind of candy to the right children at the right time. Which leads me to what has already become a crucial question: How much are you willing to pay?"

"I will pay whatever is required, provided the information we receive identifies the assassin and allows us to exercise the justice he deserves."

"Ah, Pedroso, so it is both information *and* justice that you desire! Information is one thing, but justice is another. What form of justice are you after?"

"I want two things. First, that the assassin be found; and second, that he be publicly punished, so that his sponsors or any others with similar plans understand that they can not assume immunity from politically motivated crimes no matter who is protecting them."

"I see. Well, I expect those aims may be achievable as long as the price is paid. Let me further my inquiries."

"Please."

The captain nods, pushes a buzzer on his desk, and moments later, a beautiful young secretary, her eyes and nails decorated for the night, appears with pencil and pad in hand.

"Dona Maria," the captain says, "please connect me with *Chefe Esperante*. He awaits my call."

The secretary leans over the desk, displaying the twin toys that the captain knows and loves so well, and while the captain idly pats her buttocks, she dials. She then informs someone that Capitão Barraco wishes to speak to the chefe.

After a little wait, she flashes a provocative smile at the captain, hands him the phone, and weaves her way from the room.

The conversation takes a while to complete as the captain repeatedly tries to lower the price, until finally, sitting on a corner of his desk, he says, "Good, good, thank you Francisco. I'll speak to you of this again, probably later today."

He hangs up and turns to Senhor Salles. "Pedroso, the asking price is two million. He started at three million, but dropped it to two. A favor, he claimed, born of the fact that his favorite team just won the semifinals for the World Cup. Two million is still outrageous, but he swears his expenses will take most of it. What pigshit! Still, he is dependable."

"And for two million, what do we get, João?"

"For the first million, we get the identity of the assassin, or at least that of his sponsor. He intimated that that information is already available. The assassin, I predict, will turn out to be either a policeman or a gunman who works for the police. And the sponsor will either be a group or an individual currently in power that feels threatened by popular democracy."

"And then? Once we have the identity?"

"Then, assuming the circumstances permit it—the assassin, of course, may be dead or may have fled the country—the second million will be used to arrange for appropriate justice. You shall not be troubled with that yourself. I will arrange it."

"May I inquire as to the nature …?"

"Well, there's not much by way of choice. If we arrest the assassin intending to prosecute him in the courts, his sponsors will simply bribe the judge, or even go to a higher authority and arrange his release. So legal recourse is out, leaving us to our own devices. That means that achieving justice in this case will require a Napoleonic transaction. One done publicly, in such a way as to notify the sponsor that he is or may be known—whether he is or not."

"Napoleonic . . . an eye for an eye."

"Exactly, Pedroso. Exactly."

"A crude form of justice to be sure, but one I must agree to, since as you say, we have little choice in the matter. My bank will bring you the money this afternoon."

"Fine, but don't have them bring it all. Have them bring only one million and keep the other million at the ready for when you are told that *justiça ésta realizada.* Of course, if you do not hear that justice has been realized, you should keep the second million; the first million will be gone in any case."

"Understood. And you, João, how may I recompense you?"

"Pedroso, if you continue to insult our friendship like this, I shall have to refuse to have any further dealings with you."

Senhor Salles, rising from his chair, extends a hand and says, "Then I will say no more at this time, other than to give you my heartfelt thanks, dear friend."

"It's a small favor to perform for someone to whom I owe so much, Pedroso. And now that our business is finished, let me invite you to join me tonight at the *Cabaret Quatras Meninas Bonitas* (Cabaret Four Pretty Girls.)

"I especially want to introduce you to one pretty girl who, I'm sure you'll agree, has a most interesting way of feeding one French fries. Or, if you prefer, I could invite the secretary you just saw to come along for you."

"Ah, thank you, João. You offer kindness upon kindness, but I'm unable to join you this time. I must return at once to Cafezal Tres Lagos, where a daughter in need awaits me."

The men exchange hugs, wish each other *bom futebol* (good soccer) and senhor Salles departs.

The evening of the following day, Kaede and senhor Salles are walking down a service path overlooking a valley of sugar cane, when he says, "I'm so happy to see you looking as well as you do, Kaede."

"Thank you, senhor. I hope it's not just the effect of the golden red of the evening light, but I do feel much better, now that I know Roberto's murder will be avenged."

"Provided the murderer can be found."

"I understand, senhor; but even just knowing that a serious effort is being made is helpful to me. But tell me—assuming the murderer is found—will achieving justice mean that Roberto's killer will be tried and sentenced to prison?"

"More likely it will mean that my friend will arrange some sort of improvised justice—a form of retaliation perhaps not unlike the killing of Roberto. Not the ideal solution, but as we both know, this is not a time, in our poor country, of government by law and ideals."

"I know it sounds demonic of me, senhor Salles, but in this case, I don't care about law or ideals—so long as Roberto is avenged."

"You do not sound demonic, Kaede, just grievously injured. Such a response is natural. Even God in heaven insists on revenge—purgatory or hell—for those who injure others as you have been injured. And also, it is natural, perhaps even necessary, for your future happiness that you achieve the sense of conclusion that only appropriate punishment of the assassin can create."

"Will you hear from your Federale friend soon, senhor?"

"There is no way to predict precisely, but my friend's connections are such that I expect the assassin will either be found and dealt with within a short time, or that he will not be found at all. In either case, I expect to be soon informed."

"Senhor Salles, again I thank you from the depths of my soul. I know I've asked a most difficult favor of you, and I want to tell you once more that I am ready to accede to any desires you may have regarding me, whatever they may be and whenever you may wish."

"It is too early for us to decide such things, Kaede. Let us first wait for my friend's report. Let us also wait until you recover both your physical and spiritual health sufficiently to be able to trust your own decisions. Then we may talk."

14

Justiça

One evening almost a week later, a long black Alpha Romeo, carrying three well-dressed men wearing sunglasses, pulls up to Cafezal Tres Lagos. The men step from the car and, after each takes a leisurely but careful look around, one sits on a front fender, another sits on the trunk, and the third takes a square package from the car.

Cradling the package in one arm, the man approaches the front door of the casa. As he is reaching for the knocker, the door swings open before him.

"Good evening," says senhor Salles

"Are you senhor Pedroso Salles?"

"I am."

"Your friend in Rio asked me to deliver this package, along with the message that 'justiça ésta realizada.'"

Senhor Salles grabs the package and tries to open it, but it is covered with canvas and bound with heavy twine. *I will need heavy scissors or a knife.*

"There is a further message," the man says. "It is this: 'Though the name of the subject of justiça remains unknown, it is known that he was the leader of the Loyalists of Aruja.'"

Good, Masaru will know who that is.

Eager to open the package, senhor Salles nods, says, "Thank you," and starts to close the door. The man grasps the door's edge and stops its motion.

"I was told you would have something for me as well, senhor."

"Ah yes, of course. One moment, please."

Senhor Salles places the package on a hall table and goes to his study, where he takes an envelope from a safe. Returning to the front door, he hands the envelope to the man, who opens it, quickly counts its contents, nods his satisfaction, and briskly walks back to the car.

As the men drive away, senhor Salles runs to the kitchen, grabs a knife, and slashes away the netting and canvas covering the package. Beneath the canvas, he finds a wooden box with its lid nailed shut. He thrashes through several kitchen drawers, finds a meat cleaver, and pries off the top of the box exposing a roundish object wrapped in yet more netting and canvas.

He lifts the object from the box, cuts through its cover and unwinds a long, black, blood-caked braid that had been covering the object beneath it. Startled by what he sees, he gasps and jumps back in revulsion, shouting: "Não, não! Não pode ser!"—It cannot be!

But it is. Despite the strength of his wish to deny what he sees, and despite the traumatized condition of the head in the box, he has recognized the face.

"Masaru! Masaru!" he howls. "*It was you!* Oh, oh, Masaru! Oh, oh my God!"

Dizzied by emotion, he collapses to the floor with Masaru's head coming to rest between his knees. As he sits and wails in animal distress, Kaede, returning from a walk, hears the sounds and looks in the kitchen window.

Seeing senhor Salles splayed out on the floor, she rushes into the kitchen and places protective hands on his shoulders.

"Senhor Salles, what is it!"

Dropping his hands from his face, he sits up and turns a dumbstruck face toward her, accidentally exposing the head between his legs.

"What? Who?" she exclaims in horror, and then shrieks as she recognizes the face. *"Masaru! Masaru! Oh, não!"*

She quickly scoops up the head and clasps it to her breasts. "Masaru! How? What? Tell me, senhor Salles! *Tell me who did this!"*

"It was *he!*"

"He? He?"

"It was *he*, Masaru, who killed Roberto!"

Long moments pass. Kaede vomits on her skirt, throws Masaru's head hard against a wall, and runs screaming from the house.

15

A Chorus of Hounds

A light rain drizzles through moonlit fog as men and hounds, their progress hazily traced by the lanterns, roam the hills above the lakes, calling: "dona Kaede! dona Kaede! dona Kaede!"

There is no response, save for the chorus of hounds howling in mimicry of the men. The search continues for hours, until finally senhor Salles and six workers, all of them dirty and tired, descend from the hills and approach Lago Grande.

"Look!" senhor Salles says to Kyoami. "Look here." Small shoe prints impressed in wet earth trace a path to the border of the lake where, progressing onto a slab of limestone, the prints, diminishing in size as they go, disappear just before the water.

"Be silent," says senhor Salles, "and let us listen."

The men gather the dogs and hold their muzzles and, for a while, little is heard except the distant call of a nighthawk.

Finally, senhor Salles says, "Let us hurry around the lake. Perhaps she is still walking the shore. But do not only search the shore. Also cast your lights over the water, and listen carefully. She may be wading."

Kyoami takes three men along the shore in one direction, while senhor Salles leads the others in the opposite direction. Everyone treads lightly, looking and listening, and they've not gone far when one of the men dashes to the water and, with his lantern held high, swims out into the lake.

The others watch and wait as the swimmer stops then circles around several times until water splashes on his lantern and extinguishes its flame. He then swims back in, rushes over to senhor Salles and hands him a small shoe, saying: "This was floating on the lake, senhor."

"It is hers. Was it where you stopped before you started circling?"

"Yes, senhor, it was. It was just floating there, only a few meters from shore. And after reaching it, I held my lantern up and swam in circles around the spot where I found it, looking for other signs. But I saw nothing, and then my lantern failed, so I returned to land."

"And you, Kyoami, did anyone in your group see any signs at all?"

"Não, senhor. Nada."

Senor Salles considers the situation: *It looks like she went in where we saw her footprints disappear and got as far as where he found her shoe, at a place already too deep for her to stand. But maybe the shoe drifted from closer to shore.* "All right men," he says, "Quickly now, let's complete our tour around the lake."

Within the hour, the two groups meet, having covered the entire shoreline of Lago Grande.

"Nothing again," says Kyoami before he's asked.

Senhor Salles sits on the sand. He holds his head in his hands for several minutes, then says, in a voice no one present can recognize: "She did not know how to swim."

Then after several more minutes of silence, he says: "You may all go home now. All but Kyoami. And you, Kyoami, please bring me a boat with oars and a large net. And another lantern and oil. And bring me some blankets too—I may have to spend the night."